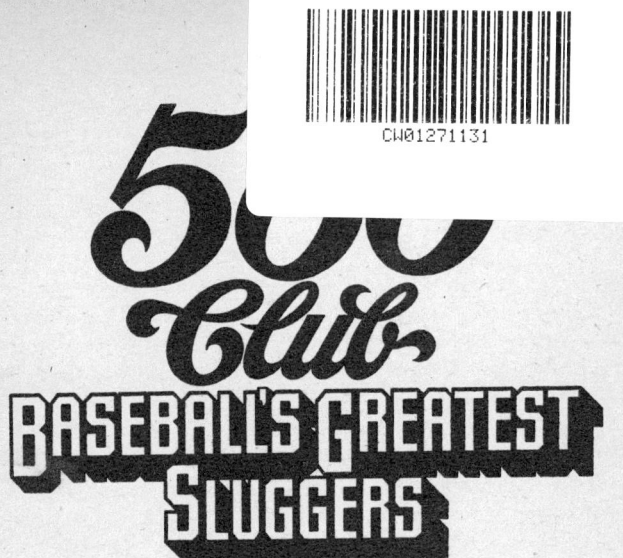

The 500 Club
Baseball's Greatest Sluggers

BART
NEW YORK

Copyright © 1988 by The Philadelphia Newspapers, Inc.

All rights reserved. No part of this book may be reproduced in any form without the written permission of the publisher.

Produced by the staff of The Philadelphia Daily News.

ISBN: 1-55785-024-0

First Bart Books edition: 1988

Bart Books
155 E. 34th Street
New York, New York 10016

Manufactured in the United States of America

Table of Contents

1. **THE HOME RUN IN BASEBALL HISTORY** — 7
   In the beginning, no longing for the long ball.
   by Rich Hofmann
2. **THE 500 CLUB** — 17
   The Slugger is baseball's preeminent figure.
   by Ray Didinger
3. **HAMMERIN' HANK AND THE BABE** — 39
   Bittersweet memories of becoming No. 1.
   by Ray Didinger
4. **500 CLUB PROFILES** — 49
   More than a bubblegum card.
   Compiled by Ray Didinger
5. **500 CLUB STATISTICS** — 67
   The numbers don't lie about this group's abilities.
6. **A SOFT SPOT FOR MASTER MELVIN** — 75
   Rooting for Mel Ott begins a pattern.
   by Stan Hochman
7. **SLUGGERS SALUTE SCHMIDT** — 81
   The latest immortal gets a warm welcome.
   by Ray Didinger
8. **A CAREER OF GREAT CLOUT** — 87
   These are the best of those 500 blasts.
   by Bill Conlin
9. **AN UNLIKELY SUPERSTAR** — 105
   In Ohio, memories of an unspectacular schoolboy.
   by Mark Kram
10. **VICTIMS OF THE HOME RUN** — 115
    How it feels to hurl oneself into history.
    by Paul Domowitch
11. **HOME RUN HEYDAY** — 121
    The big boppers of the '50s and '60s.
    by Bernard Fernandez

Table of Contents

1. **THE HOME RUN IN BASEBALL HISTORY** 1
   In the beginning, no dreams of the long ball.
   by John Thorn

2. **THE BIG BATS** 13
   The slugger in baseball's preeminent figure.
   by Ray Robinson

3. **HANK AARON AND THE BABE** 29
   Discusses the moment of becoming No. 1.
   by Ray Gamper

4. **GOD BLESS FOOT RES** 59
   More than a bothering coach.
   Compiled by Ray Robinson

5. **GOD CLUB STATISTICS** 67
   The numbers that I've used this great subject.

6. **A BEST SHOT FOR MASTER MELVIN** 75
   Batting for .325 defines me a pitcher.
   by Fred Graham

7. **ZUIDARTS AGAIN'T SABBOT** 81
   The little Brooklyn gets a home on losing.
   by Ray Robinson

8. **A MASTER OF GREAT CHEF** 87
   These are the best of there 500 blasts.
   by Bill Stone

9. **AN UNUSUAL SUPERSTAR** 105
   It takes imagination of an ultracomplex accounting.
   by Peter Drum

10. **VICTIMS OF THE HOME RUN** 115
    Even a losing is bad himself into history.
    by Paul Dornstein

11. **HOME RUN KEVDAY** 121
    was the foxie—everyone said that poscent pla...
    by George Vannett, 7

THE HOME RUN IN BASEBALL HISTORY

BY RICH HOFMANN

This is not the usual sports writing hyperbole. This is honest-to-goodness fact. Baseball was revolutionized in two years, 1920 and 1921. The game never has changed more in such a short period of time. Never.

In those two years, baseball discovered the home run. There are a lot of reasons why baseball waited so long to fall in love with the long ball. There are a lot of reasons why the changes happened so rapidly. Read on for details, but remember for now that it was those rapid changes, in those long-ago seasons, that made it possible for Mike Schmidt to reach the summit. And there are only two things to think about:
- The ball.
- And, the Babe.

■

Seeking a point of reference, a pre-1920 point of reference, we offer John J. McGraw. He played for the Baltimore Orioles in the 1890s along with people like Wee Willie Keeler. Those Orioles were credited with inventing a lot of today's "inside baseball" techniques like the hit-and-run and the squeeze play. Later, McGraw was a manager for 33 years (30 with the New York Giants). He managed teams that went to nine World Series, managed himself right into the Hall of Fame. In all, a fine point of reference.

McGraw was writing in a 1919 issue of a magazine entitled, simply, *Baseball*. Back in the old days—for him, that was the 1890s—McGraw said that baseball players were chosen for their size and brawn, like football players. But that changed.

"The old type of ball-player died out pretty largely in those years when the Orioles were the pick of the circuit [the late '90s]," McGraw wrote. "I was one of those who drove them out of the game. The managers came to realize that speed was quite as important as bulk, and that a little man was not only much faster than a human elephant, but that he could hit quite as often if not as hard.

"The passing of the home-run hitters was a good thing, for it made the game faster and flashier," McGraw wrote.

So, there is your reference. Baseball people *did not like* home runs. That seems like an incredible statement, but it was true. Baseball people did not think that hitting the ball over the fence was the way the game should be played. As late as 1910-15, some sports writers referred to inside-the-park homers as "real" or "bonafide" home runs. The clear implication was that home runs hit over the fence somehow weren't as good.

The genesis of this attitude is unclear. It is possible—and McGraw's words seem to bear this out—that the people back then found the finesse game to be more aesthetically pleasing. It is possible that a bloop single to the opposite field, followed by a stolen base, followed by a sacrifice bunt, followed by a sacrifice fly, was thought to be more exciting than a home run. Maybe they liked the way that it fostered a sense of teamwork, seeing as how even the big stars like Ty Cobb were expected to sacrifice and things like that for the good of the team.

Or maybe, the attitude sprung from the facts of baseball life back then. The facts, specifically, involved the ball and what the pitcher could do with it.

■ The ball: It always has been the same size, and the same weight. But in the days before 1920, it just didn't go anywhere. Ruth referred to it derisively as a "squash," quickly forgetting the days when he used to pitch, and not hit, for a living.

■ The pitcher: Before 1920, he could do all kinds of things to the ball, artificial things that made it dive and sail erratically. The most noteworthy tactic, of course, was the spitball.

The spitter, it is generally agreed, was first used by Elmer Stricklett, who pitched for Chicago of the American League and Brooklyn of the National League between 1904 and 1907. Others, though, became more proficient. Two that come to mind were Jack Chesbro and Ed Walsh.

The emery ball and the shine ball were different, but the principle was the same. Anything done to the ball's cover—roughing it up with emery paper, shining it on the uniform, secretly applying a dab of wax to it, cutting it on the belt-buckle—caused the ball to behave erratically. Some of those things also made it tough to see.

Nevertheless, whether it was the ball, or the pitchers, or the general attitude, baseball before 1920 was really different. And the home run wasn't really a part of it.

In 1908, Sam Crawford, of the Detroit Tigers, won the American League home run championship. Crawford hit seven homers that year. One of the great inappropriate nicknames was the one used by Frank "Home Run" Baker. In 1913, he had his biggest home run year—12.

Until Babe Ruth changed everything, only two players had hit more than 20 homers in a season—Frank "Wildfire" Schulte, of the Cubs, had 21 in 1911 and Gavvy Cravath, of the Phillies, had 24 in 1915.

Then, boom.

There was no subtlety, and almost no warning. But in 1919, in his last year with the Boston Red Sox, Babe Ruth pretty much stopped pitching and headed for the outfield. And there, he stunned the baseball world by hitting 29 home runs, a new record.

This was big stuff. World War I was over, people were looking for some fun, and Ruth became a sideshow. Twenty-nine homers! Imagine!

Harry Frazee, the Red Sox' owner, needed money. So he sold Ruth to the Yankees for the unheard-of sum of $125,000. And, in his first year with the Yankees, Ruth hit 54 homers.

Fifty-four!

Boom.

But it wasn't only Ruth. Check out the numbers. Robert Creamer, one of Ruth's biographers, points out these:

"It was not a gradual evolution but sudden and cataclysmic. Baseball statistics give dramatic evidence of this. For fifteen seasons before 1919, major league batters as a group averaged around .250. By 1921 that figure had jumped above .285, and it remained steadily in the .280s throughout the 1920s . . . Before 1920 it was a rare year when more than two or three men in both leagues batted in 100 runs; but in 1921 fifteen players did it, and the average for the 1920s was fourteen a year . . . Before 1919 the average annual ERA was about 2.85. In 1921 it was over 4.00, and it stayed in that generous neighborhood through the decade.

"What caused the explosion?" Creamer asked.

It was an oft-asked question, as balls flew out of ballparks at an unprecedented rate. Even without Ruth's numbers, there were about 50 percent more homers in the American League in 1920 than there were in 1919. They flew out so frequently that people soon forgot about the Black Sox scandal of 1919, about the fixed World Series between Chicago and Cincinnati.

On June 4, 1920, the Philadelphia A's hit seven home runs in a single game at Shibe Park against the Detroit Tigers. At the time, it was a record. As the *Inquirer* reported the next day, "It was one of the glorious days of swat."

Again, why?

Again, two reasons: The ball, and the Babe.

Ruth clearly was a big part of it. His 29 homers in 1919, according to more than one theory, greatly impressed baseball's owners. Then, as now, anything that made them more money impressed baseball's owners. And Babe Ruth was making them more money. Home runs sold, tradition or not.

So, according to the theory, the owners sought a way to increase home run production throughout the majors. And that's why—again, according to the theory—the owners decided to ban the spitball, the emery ball, the shine ball, and any other "freak" pitch. Only pitchers who regularly used the spitter—and no more than two per team—were allowed to continue. Attrition got rid of them all by 1934, when Burleigh Grimes tossed his last wet one.

The owners also juiced up the ball. They had to have done

something, even though they would never admit it. Thomas Shibe—the park was named after his family—was vice president of the Philadelphia A's and a member of the firm that manufactured baseballs for the major leagues. In June of 1920, as the rockets flew out, he denied that the ball had been souped up.

"The baseball used this year is the same as used last year and several years before that," he said. "The specifications this year called for the same yarn, the same cork centre, the same size and weight of rubber and the same horsehide. It has not been changed one iota and no effort has been made to turn out a livelier ball . . .

"With all the freak deliveries dead, and the spitter almost dead, the batsmen are able to hit the ball more solidly," Shibe said.

Over the years, many people have speculated about the change made in 1920. There was talk about a better grade of horsehide. There also was talk of American wool yarn being replaced by a tighter, stronger brand of yarn from Australia. But, as Creamer has written, "No hard irrefutable facts exist to verify this—indeed, a laboratory test in August 1920 'proved' the ball had not been changed . . ."

But the numbers did not lie.

Something happened.

■

This was a big deal, and observers of the game recognized the radical change almost immediately. It was all over the newspapers for two consecutive summers, 1920 and '21. The word "furor" was used more than once. Like here, from The *New York Times:*

"In the furor that has been raised of late against the home-run hitting, one fact seems to have been generally overlooked. This is the part which the various fields play in the long-distance hitting. Much is heard about the lively ball and the rules which handicap the pitchers, but the critics have been paying little or no attention to the fact that banging homers has been a matter of locality to a great extent."

The teams that led in homers were those from both leagues that played in New York, St. Louis, and Philadelphia. At the time, both the New York teams played at the Polo Grounds, where the rightfield fence was 257 feet, 8 inches away. In St. Louis, it was Sportsman's Park, where the rightfield bleachers were 310 feet from the plate. And then there was Philadelphia.

The A's played at Shibe Park, later to be named Connie Mack Stadium. That was a normal-sized stadium, 331 feet to the rightfield flagpole. But the Phillies played at the Baker Bowl, and the rightfield fence there was the joke of all time. It is unclear from the clippings just how short it was in 1920. But it was bad enough that home plate was moved back and the field refigured in 1925.

The new, improved distance?

All of 280 feet, 6 inches.

So, maybe the parks did contribute. Whatever. The fact is, the home run was now part of the game. Striking out was no longer a disgrace, if it was done in pursuit of the big knock. Teams now could sit and wait for the big inning. Stolen base totals fell.

The fans clearly loved it, but some people were never won over. Here is the great pitcher, Christy Mathewson, writing in The *New York Times* in 1920:

"There seems to be a great demand these days for star sluggers. There is no doubt of their value to a team, and a man who can rap out a home run frequently furnishes the fans with the most spectacular play in the game.

"But from the point of view of winning contests, my experience has taught me to prefer an aggregation of good base runners to a batting order of hard hitters. I believe the former can do more to help a pitcher win games."

Other people were ridiculously opposed to the new game, almost hysterically so. *Literary Digest*—in summarizing an article written by someone named Irving E. Sanborn in *Baseball* magazine—carried this headline: "Baseball Shuddering at the Home Run Menace." It said that "there were so many home runs last summer [1923]—so many, in fact, that the popularity of baseball is said to be facing something like a crisis."

Sanborn argued against the "cheapening" of the home run. He thought the people would get sick of homers. He said, "There is no more tempting appeal to an epicurean appetite than quail done to a turn and served hot. But history does not record the fact that anyone has yet been able to inhale thirty quail in thirty days without nausea."

This Sanborn guy really had his finger on the pulse. A lot of people probably threw up when Ruth hit 60 homers in 1927.

And then, some people laughed. Here is Walter Dunn, a columnist for the old Philadelphia *Public Ledger:*

"It is dangerous these days to sleep at a big league game," he wrote. ". . . Any man or woman who falls into the land of slumber in the days of lively baseball takes a chance of never awakening . . . Since the baseballs are made of horsehide it appears as though speed has been taken from Man o' War."

But behind these jokes, there was a truth.

"Lively baseball has caused the thoughts of the fans to drift far, far away from the 1919 World Series scandal," Dunn wrote. "Home runs make up the big ideas of the great American game. The paying public would rather hear of a circuit clout from the bats of such overpaid athletes as Babe Ruth, George Kelly, and others than renew thoughts" of the Black Sox scandal.

Almost seven decades later, managers wait for home runs. Oh, people still hit and run, still steal bases, still do all of that John McGraw "inside baseball" stuff. But when you talk offense, you talk long ball.

Listen to Earl Weaver, a zealot on the subject:

"I've got nothing against the bunt—in its place. But most of the time that place is the bottom of a long-forgotten closet. Forget about the bunt unless there is no other choice. Look instead to Dr. Longball and his assistant, Dr. Three-Hit. Those are the best friends of any manager, and they can make a team healthy in a hurry. The home run makes managing simple . . . The power of the home run is so elementary that I fail to comprehend why people try to outsmart this game in other ways."

And now, springing from that kind of environment, we have Mike Schmidt hitting his 500th home run.

A lot already has been written and said about the accomplishment. It is a monument to a man and to his career. But it

is also a reminder of a time long ago. It is another chapter in a baseball reformation, another affirmation of what might be the sport's most significant revolution.
  Remember 1920.

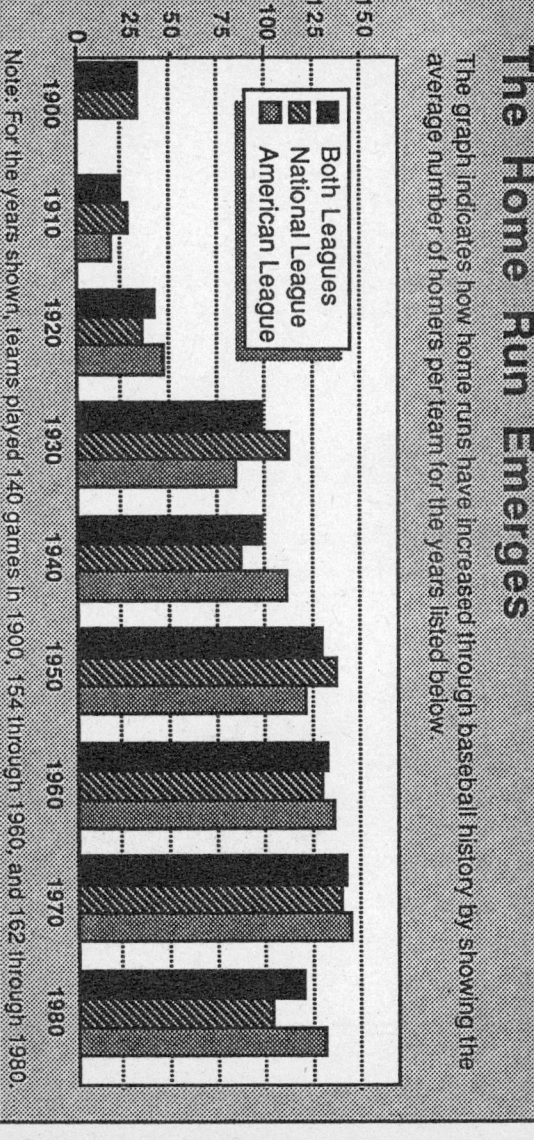

In baseball, very few people achieve true career milestones. Such marks are attained only by those with a rare combination of ability and longevity. Pitchers strive for 300 victories. Hitters go after 3,000 hits. For sluggers, the number in the distance is 500.

THE 500 CLUB

BY RAY DIDINGER

We stand in awe of The Slugger. He is part-man, part-myth, and All-American. He is the heavy-weight champion of our national pastime, Paul Bunyan with a 36-ounce switch. He swings hard, he hits hard and even when he fails, he fails hard. It is all part of the mystique.

The Mighty Casey, now there was a Slugger. He struck out and they still wrote a poem about him. Roy Hobbs, "The Natural," was another one.

Did you ever notice there aren't any literary classics devoted to singles hitters or middle relievers? It is always the man who carries the big stick. That is because The Slugger is a special breed.

We can all close our eyes and make a lucky catch. Given enough chances, we can all throw a strike. But we can't all hit a baseball over the roof at Yankee Stadium. We can only dream it, and, of course, we do.

The Slugger does it for real—usually in the bottom of the ninth, with a 3-2 count—and we are days trying to catch our breath.

"How does he do it?" we wonder.

There is no mystery in a 7-4 Ralph Sampson dropping a basketball through a hoop. Or, for that matter, a 240-pound Larry Csonka running over a 170-pound tackler.

But what is it that enables a man no bigger than your next-door neighbor to drive a baseball 540 feet into the centerfield bleachers? Not just once, mind you, but over and over again.

Say, 35 times a year for 15 years. Say, 500 times, total.

What is it that allows a Mike Schmidt to become one of just 14 major leaguers to reach that milestone? What is it that sets the 500 Home Run Clubber apart from every other Class A prospect who ever wrapped his dreams around a Louisville Slugger?

That is the fascination of the home run fraternity. That is why we chase after these men with our note pads and tape measures. That is why we cast them in bronze and give them nicknames—the Babe, the Hammer, the Beast, the Killer—suitable for a legend.

"When you think about it, the home run is the ultimate analogy," said Reggie Jackson, the former Cheltenham High School star who has announced his retirement after last season with 563 career home runs. His total ranks sixth all-time.

"When people want to describe a great feeling," Jackson said, "they don't say, 'It was like serving an ace at Wimbledon.' They don't say, 'It was like making a hole-in-one at the Masters.' They don't say, 'It was like winning the Indy 500.' They say, 'It was like hitting a homer in the World Series.'

"Why? Because baseball is a game we can all relate to. It's the American game. And the power . . . who doesn't dream about power? I know that's what I love about hitting. It's a show of strength.

"It's two against one at the plate, the pitcher and the catcher vs. you. When I'm up there I'm thinking, 'Try everything you want. Rub up the ball. Move the fielders around. I'm still gonna hit that ball.' God, do I love to hit that ball outta the park and hear 'em say, 'Wow.'

"That," Jackson said, "is what it's all about, that moment. Really, there are no words to describe it. But I'll tell you this: You could do it 500 times—or 5,000 times—and it would never get old."

Indeed, there is no athletic feat so neatly defined, no moment of triumph quite so focused as the home run.

All eyes follow the majestic flight of the ball, then return to The Slugger as he circles the bases. The stage is his alone.

The game has stopped. Nothing more can happen until he allows it to happen.

With a single stroke, The Slugger has electrified an entire stadium, not to mention a vast TV and radio audience. He has put his stamp on the contest. And there were no downfield blocks, no assists, no helping hands of any kind.

Just The Slugger and his bat. That is the beauty of it and it has not changed in almost a century.

That is what we pay to see and that is what we talk about the next day at work. "You should've seen it . . . You should've *heard* it . . . That ball must have gone 500 feet, at least." OK, so maybe it went 400. Who's counting?

"Do you think about hitting them far?" a newsman once asked Babe Ruth, the man who established the home run as a staple of American culture.

"Well, kid," the Babe replied. "I don't think about hitting 'em short."

That is what made the Babe the Babe, the Hammer the Hammer and Schmitty, well, Schmitty. And we wouldn't have it any other way.

■

It is baseball's select circle, the 500 Home Run Club. It is the prestige address in Cooperstown, N.Y., an executive suite within the Hall of Fame.

Consider the men who *don't* belong: Lou Gehrig (493), Stan Musial and Willie Stargell (475), Carl Yastrzemski (452) and Duke Snider (407). Joltin' Joe DiMaggio didn't even come close (361).

Great players every one, but they still could not get past the doorman at Club 500. That, folks, is what you call an exclusive membership.

Michael Jack Schmidt now has been formally welcomed. He joins Mel Ott (511), Ernie Banks and Eddie Mathews (512), Ted Williams and Willie McCovey (521), Jimmie Foxx (534), Mickey Mantle (536), Jackson (563), Harmon Killebrew (573) and Frank Robinson (586).

Willie Mays is a notch above at 660. Ruth had the record they said would never be broken: 714 home runs. Then there is Hank Aaron, the Hammer, who surpassed the Babe and now stands alone at 755.

That is 14 men in more than 100 years of baseball.

"I don't think you'll see 14 more," said California manager Gene Mauch. "You might not see four more. How many guys come along with that combination of power, consistency and longevity? You're talking about guys who play at another level."

Agreed, but what was it that made these men tick? Do they have something in common aside from keen eyes and quick hands? Did I say keen eyes? Scratch that. Reggie Jackson wears glasses. His eyes are as bad as Ted Williams's eyes are good.

OK, so what is it?

Physically, there are similarities. Ten of the 14 are within an inch of 6-foot tall. Most weighed around 190 pounds. Killebrew, Jackson, Foxx, and Mantle are listed at 6-foot, 195, although Foxx (he was the Beast) was probably a little heftier.

Ott was the smallest at 5-9, 170. McCovey, better known as "Stretch," was the tallest at 6-4. It should come as no surprise to learn Ruth was the heaviest. The Hall of Fame records list the Babe at 6-2, 215, but that was probably his weight as a Boston Red Sox rookie.

During his glory years with the Yankees, the Babe was lugging around at least 230 pounds and that's not counting the blonde on each arm. His appetite, in every area, was legendary.

As you might expect, all 14 men were superb all-around athletes. The 11 modern-era sluggers starred in football as well as baseball in high school. It was football, in fact, that led to the knee problems that haunted Mantle and Schmidt throughout their major league careers.

Killebrew was one of the nation's top high school quarterbacks as a senior in Payette, Idaho. Jackson was a halfback with 9.6 speed who went to Arizona State on a football scholarship. Mathews passed up a football scholarship to Georgia to sign a $6,000 contract with the Boston Braves in 1949.

"I signed at my senior prom, one minute after midnight," recalled Mathews, now a minor league hitting instructor with the Braves. "I was tired of school and my dad was sick [tuberculosis]. Six thousand was a lot of money back then."

Ernie Banks was an end in football and high-jumper (5 feet, 11 inches) in track. McCovey set a school record with 11 varsity letters in Mobile, Ala. And to this day, Willie Mays insists football, not baseball, was his best sport in high school.

"I was a quarterback," Mays said recently. "I could run the ball, throw the ball. Whatever you want, I could do. Football was my game but the [bonus] money was in baseball so that's where I went. Can't say I regret it now."

They weren't huge men even among their major league peers. There were other players with wider shoulders and bigger biceps—guys like Ted Kluszewski, Frank Howard, and Boog Powell—but they didn't come close to the 500 class. They had the power but not the consistency.

Make no mistake: Strength is a necessary part of the equation. We think of Banks as a wispy 6-1, 175-pound shortstop but he had the wrists and forearms of a blacksmith. "You grab a hold of him," former Cubs manager Bob Scheffing said, "and it's like grabbing steel."

Aaron was rather average in appearance at 6-foot, 180 pounds, yet he hit the ball harder more often than anyone who ever played the game. He never lifted a weight, but he hit 40 or more home runs eight times in his major league career.

Aaron's secret, if you could call it that, was his wrists. You could make the same statement about most of the 500 Clubbers. Even a big stud such as McCovey relied more on timing and quick hands than muscle to drive balls through the wind at Candlestick Park.

"Willie's hands travel with lightning speed for about a foot and a half," former Giants manager Bill Rigney said. "He packs the power of a good boxer's right hand. It is sudden and explosive . . . boom."

"People got fooled by Hank Aaron's follow-through and his distance," Mauch said. "They assumed he took a big cut. He didn't. His swing was really from here to here [roughly the length of home plate].

"He didn't get that nickname 'Hammer' for nothing. He

hammered that ball, he chopped down on it. That's what you call power-hitting. The players today have these big, long swings. All that's doing is making them slow [with the bat]."

Former Pittsburgh pitcher Bob Friend agrees. "Those wrist hitters don't have the weaknesses other hitters have," Friend said. "It's fantastic how long Henry can look at a pitch. It's like giving him an extra strike.

"The best thing you can do is keep the ball where he'll only hit singles."

Aaron's power figures are stunning. He is the all-time major league leader in total bases (6,856), extra base hits (1,477) and RBI (2,297) as well as home runs.

But what often is overlooked is Aaron's .305 career batting average. He won two National League batting titles in the '50s. He was a tougher out then because he hit the ball to all fields. When the Braves moved to Atlanta in 1966, Aaron went for power and tried to pull everything.

Early in his career, Aaron's teammates marveled at how he never seemed to crack a bat. He went through a half-season using the same 33-ounce Louisville Slugger. No one could understand it.

One day Warren Spahn examined the bat and found all the dents—the places where Aaron had hit the ball—were in the same "sweet" part. In other words, Aaron never got jammed or fooled by a pitch. His concentration and bat control were virtually flawless.

"The amazing thing about Henry was he made [hitting] look so easy," said Matthews, who combined with Aaron to hit 863 homers for the Braves, surpassing Ruth and Gehrig as the most potent 1-2 punch in baseball history.

"Henry would look so loose and relaxed at the plate. You almost never saw him grinding the bat handle. Then the pitch would come in and he'd just uncoil. We had a friendly rivalry about who would hit more [homers] and Henry usually got the better of me.

"But it was just a pleasure to watch that man handle a bat. He looked like an orchestra conductor with his baton, you know, just that smooth."

Babe Ruth was not a wrist hitter. He believed in taking a lusty whack at the ball, putting all his weight into it. Sometimes the Babe fell down after a swinging strike. No problem. He would simply adjust his cap and take a similar cut at the next pitch.

Mel Ott was famous for his exaggerated stride. A left-handed hitter, Ott would raise his right leg to knee-height as the pitcher was in his windup, then Ott would step down just before impact. It looked funny but it worked just fine. Ott won the National League home run title six times.

Of the recent 500 Clubbers, Jackson is the closest thing to an old-school slugger. He swings savagely and often in futility. Jackson added to his lead as the major league's career leader in strikeouts in 1987. He has 2,597.

If that sounds like a lot, it is. That is more strikeouts as Ruth and Banks combined (2,566). But another way: Reggie has more strikeouts than the Yankees' Don Mattingly has at-bats. The straw that stirs the drink also stirs a lot of air.

The 500 Club accounts for seven of the top 14 all-time strikeout victims. Schmidt is fifth with 1,744. Aaron's strikeout ratio was a modest one for every 8.9 at-bats.

Among the great power hitters, only Ted Williams was tougher to fan. The Splendid Splinter struck out once for every 10.8 at-bats. Even more remarkable, Williams retired with almost three times as many walks (2,019, No. 2 behind Ruth) as strikeouts. That is unheard of.

Williams put his baseball philosophy in a 1960 book entitled, *The Science of Hitting*. It still is considered the definitive thesis on the subject. Williams stresses the need for the batter to be selective, "to get a good ball to hit."

"A good hitter can hit a pitch that is over the plate three times better than a great hitter with a questionable ball in a tough spot," Williams wrote. "Pitchers still make enough mistakes to give you some in your 'happy zone.' But the greatest hitter living can't hit bad balls good."

You might want to circle that last sentence and leave it in Juan Samuel's locker.

"When you start fishing for the pitch that's an inch off the plate," Williams wrote, "the pitcher—if he's smart—will put the next one 2 inches off. Then 3. And before you know it, you're making 50 outs a year on pitches you never should have swung at."

Williams was the Morris the Cat of 500 Clubbers: he was finicky about his pitches. That is why he retired after 19 seasons with a .344 average, sixth best all-time and just one point behind the ultimate Punch-and-Judy hitter, Wee Willie Keeler.

"Takes all kinds, you know?" Willie Mayes said. "Ted Williams wrote a book about hitting and I couldn't write a *page*. Hitting was just something I did naturally.

"I couldn't teach you how to hit home runs anymore than I could teach you how to jump off the roof and fly. Certain folks, God just made to hit. Williams was born to hit but he spent a whole lot of time thinking about it. I never did.

"People say I hit a lot of bad balls for home runs," Mays said, giggling. "I say, 'Well, they were bad until I hit them. Then they got good.'"

■

If there is a common thread in the 500 Home Run Club, it is that the members arrived at the major leagues with a fair amount of dirt under their fingernails.

None of them had a butler to pitch them batting practice when they were kids, In other words. Schmidt grew up in a middle-class family in Dayton, Ohio. The other 13 players, particularly the blacks, saw their share of hard times.

Aaron and McCovey grew up in Mobile, Ala., although they hardly knew each other back then. Aaron's father earned $75 a week as a boilermaker's helper. McCovey's dad worked on the railroad.

Banks lived in Dallas where his father was a warehouse porter. Ernie's first baseball glove cost $2.98. Mays went to an industrial school in Westfield, Ala., where he was trained as a laundry presser. He decided to sign with the Birmingham Black Barons of the Negro League, instead.

"My father told me to stay away from the factory as long as I could," Mays recalled. "He said, 'Son, you take one of those jobs and you're a goner,' He was right, too."

Jackson lived with his divorced father, a tailor in Wyncote. Foxx worked on a farm in Sudlersville, Md. Williams was raised by his mother, a clarinet player in the Salvation Army band near San Diego. Mantle earned $35 a week as a teenager digging in the zinc mine near his Oklahoma home.

Tough roads, all of them. The one thing that brought these 14 very different men together was their gift for hitting a baseball. It was that skill that brought them fame and wealth, but learning how to deal with that wasn't easy.

A few, such as Ruth and Jackson, had personalities that seemed to flourish with the attention. Others, such as Schmidt, Killebrew, Mays, McCovey, and Banks, grew into the role after some initial discomfort.

Mathews never did like the spotlight. He was that way as a Boston Braves rookie in 1952 and he didn't change in 17 seasons as a player. He had to open up a little when he served as the Braves' manager [1972 to '74] but it didn't get any easier.

"I was from the old school . . . I'd tell them, 'You saw it, you write it,' " Mathews said.

"[Newsmen] were always asking, 'How did this feel?' and 'How did that feel?' I didn't know what to say. If we won, I felt good. If we lost, I felt horsebleep. End of story. But I guess they wanted more.

"They paid me to play this game, not analyze it. I got off to a good start [72 homers his first two seasons] and got a lot of attention. I was just 22, shy as hell. I didn't like talking about myself but it came out like I was a bad guy.

"That's the trouble with being at that level," Mathews said. "Everything you do becomes magnified. I steered clear of that pretty much, but I saw it eat other guys alive."

After awhile, the daily pressure of living in a fishbowl got to most of the great sluggers. Even Jackson, a man who sucks up adulation the way a thirsty lawn sucks up water, is known to snap when the 500th autograph book of the day is shoved through his car window.

Mickey Mantle came to New York a quiet, wide-eyed kid of 21, fresh from the zinc mine. It didn't take long for him to develop a hard edge in dealing with the public. The first one to write about the Mick's dark side was teammate Jim Bouton in his tell-all book, *Ball Four*.

"There were . . . times when [Mantle] would push little kids aside when they wanted his autograph," Bouton wrote, "and times when he was snotty to reporters, just about making them crawl and beg for a minute of his time. I've seen him close a bus window on kids trying to get his autograph.

"And I don't like the Mantle that refused to sign baseballs in the clubhouse before games. Everybody else had to sign, but Little Pete [the clubhouse man] forged Mantle's signature. So there are thousands of baseballs around the country that have been signed not by Mickey Mantle but by Pete Previte."

Mantle might have been tough to deal with at times but he was an absolute prince compared to Ted Williams. It wasn't unusual for Williams to spit at an unruly fan or answer a loud boo with an obscene gesture. His own general manager, Joe Cronin, referred to the rookie Williams as "that busher."

Wrote Harry Ober in the New York *Mirror*: "The public image of Williams has been that of an acid-tongue, frequently obscene, sputtering and often vulgar man. In a word, unlovable."

What could be more unlovable than a man who hits a poor old lady in the head with a baseball bat? That is what Williams did in 1958 when he hurled his bat in disgust after popping up in the ninth inning.

Williams's bat flew 75 feet and struck Gladys Heffernan, 69, the housekeeper for Cronin. She was OK but she asked Cronin to get her tickets in the upper deck after that.

Even Williams was remorseful over that display of temper. He never again threw his bat into the stands. He held onto it and smashed the water cooler, instead.

"Ted was, at times, a victim of his own intensity," said Frank Malzone, a former Boston teammate, now a Red Sox minor league instructor. "He worked so hard at his game and took such pride in his performance that he couldn't just shrug off an 0-for-4 the way most guys do.

"I didn't join the team until later [1955] when Ted's career was winding down. He had mellowed by then. He was still feuding with the writers in Boston, but he wasn't the [terror] he was in his early years. Basically, Ted just didn't want to be bothered.

"That's where the problems start for all these [superstars]. They are decent enough guys but they are under that pressure all the time. Not just pressure to perform on the field, but to do interviews, sign autographs, the whole bit.

"Most I know don't have the patience for it," Malzone said. "Ted didn't. He just wanted to work on his hitting and fish. He didn't have that much to say unless you were talking about those two things."

Williams, now 68, is more easygoing these days. He spends spring training with the Bosox in Winter Haven, Fla., working with the minor league hitters and chatting with the fans. He even talks to the writers, a sure sign the old Thumper is at peace with the world.

To a man, the retired 500 Home Run Clubbers reflect a kind of blissful serenity. Their place in baseball history is secure; they know that.

Five-hundred home runs is not an achievement that will be diluted in time. We're not talking about a one-shot deal like the 4-minute mile or the 1,000-yard season in football. Any athlete can have one great day or season, but 500 home runs requires two great *decades*.

That is the stuff of legends and the 11 living 500 Clubbers, counting Schmidt, fully appreciate that fact. They might not say it, but they know they always will be considered baseball royalty. It is a nice, warm feeling to carry into middle age.

"I never thought much about what I was doing while I was doing it," the 56-year-old Mays said this spring. He was in the Giants' camp in Scottsdale, Ariz., along with McCovey, as a "special assistant" to club president Al Rosen.

"I didn't worry about my 100th home run, my 200th home run and junk like that," Mays said. "The only one I paid much attention to was No. 512. That broke Mel Ott's record [national league] at the time. But even then I predicted Aaron would pass me before he was done.

"I passed some great hitters on my way up the ladder. Gehrig, Musial, Kiner, people like that. But I didn't take the time to appreciate it because there was always another game the next day. I had enough confidence in my own ability, I knew if I just played the game, the numbers would be there.

"The satisfaction comes now, when I see how people react to what I did. I've seen [former manager] Leo Durocher quoted as saying I was the best player he ever saw. Frank

Robinson, a man I respect to the utmost, said something similar. That means more to me than a lot of trophies and clippings."

"It bothers me when a rookie has a good year and they refer to him as a 'superstar,'" Willie McCovey said. "That cheapens the meaning of the word. One year is just that, one year. A superstar is a player who stands the test of time.

"I don't know how many centerfielders I've seen compared to Willie Mays. We've had six right here [with the Giants]. You'd think people would learn after awhile. There will never be another Willie Mays. There will never be another Aaron . . ."

"Will there ever be another McCovey?" a visitor asked.

A smile spread slowly across McCovey's face.

"Well, I've never been the kind of man who boasts," he said. He paused and stared across the empty clubhouse. The Giants players were on the field loosening up for the morning intrasquad game. Old No. 44 would be along directly.

"Let me put it this way," McCovey said. "I always felt I belonged with the best. I played alongside Mays, I played against Musial, Snider, Mantle, Robinson. I didn't feel I had to take a back seat to anybody. I just didn't brag like some.

"I knew how the other players felt about me. I had guys tell me, 'Man, you're too good for this league. You're in a league all your own.' Banks told me if I played in Wrigley Field, I'd hit 80 home runs a year. I said, 'Yeah, you're probably right.'

"I never said too much to anyone—sports writers, other players, anybody—because it wasn't my nature. I also liked to keep a little air of mystery about myself. Pitchers weren't quite sure how I'd react if they came inside on me so they left me alone.

"Mays, he fraternized all the time. He'd spend an hour joking [with the other team] around the batting cage. Then he'd get knocked down three times during the game. I got a little edge by keeping my distance."

Reggie Jackson had a different kind of mystique during his five seasons in New York. He fraternized with the opposing team largely because he could not fraternize with his own. He was, in the words of former teammate Elrod Hendricks, "an outcast" in Yankee-land.

"I'd describe Reggie as a combination of Muhammad Ali and Frank Robinson," said Hendricks, now the bullpen coach in Baltimore. "He was a great self-promoter, which rubbed a lot of players the wrong way. But he was also a great competitor like Robby. He knew how to win.

"I was with that [1977 Yankee] team so I know how Reggie was received. There was a very strong veteran nucleus and those guys just never accepted Reggie. He didn't help matters with a few of his statements [most notably, the famous "I-am-the-straw-that-stirs-the-drink" line] but he produced."

"What made Reggie so great was he never let anything get in his way," said Oakland coach Joe Rudi, Jackson's former A's teammate. "He never had a wife or family [he was divorced early]. His whole life was baseball and he put everything he had into it.

"He was a showman, that's true, but he seemed to thrive on the controversy. The hotter things got, the better he performed. It would be interesting to see how many of his home runs came in the eighth and ninth innings. I'll bet it was a bunch."

"That's confidence," Jackson said. "I've been in that situation so many times, I know how to handle it. The pitcher knows that and maybe he's a little more nervous than he would be ordinarily.

"If you can win that battle of the minds, chances are you'll win that battle at the plate, too."

■

Mike Schmidt brings with him to the 500 Club an impressive collection of 10 Gold Gloves. He is a complete player, which pleases his new fraternity brothers no end.

They would not be terribly thrilled to see a one-dimensional figure such as Dave Kingman waddle into their midst. Call them old-fashioned, but the 500 gang takes pride in the fact it could play the game . . .

The *whole* game.

OK, Reggie Jackson was no gazelle in the outfield and, granted, Ted Williams's mind seemed to wander when he didn't have a bat in his hands. It is true Harmon Killebrew stole just 19 bases in 22 major league seasons but, really, that's nit-picking.

The fact is, Jackson and Williams never were less than adequate defensively and Killebrew, although slow of foot, played first base, third, and the outfield for Minnesota. In his *Baseball Abstract,* Bill James ranked Killebrew as the second most valuable multiposition player of all-time, behind Pete Rose.

Willie McCovey is often thought of as a gangly first baseman who was employed strictly for his bat, but the fact is McCovey made himself into a solid major league glove man. Stretch also played the outfield and once saved a Juan Marichal no-hitter with a diving catch that robbed Houston's Carl Warwick of extra bases.

"We all get stuck with labels, mine was the big brute," McCovey said. "But I wasn't like [Dick] Stuart and [Steve] Bilko or Kingman today. I could do a lot of things on a ballfield. I would have done more if I didn't have so many [knee] injuries.

"But I look at Aaron, Mays, and Robinson, they deserved all the credit they got. Mays was the best ever, in my opinion, and I saw him every day for 13 years. People would ask me, 'What's the one play [by Mays] that stands out in your mind?' Who could pick out *one* play by Willie Mays?"

Folks who followed the Giants in 1954—that's five years before McCovey came aboard—would have no trouble picking out one play. It was Mays's breathtaking, over-the-shoulder catch against Cleveland's Vic Wertz in the '54 World Series.

It might be the most talked-about defensive play in baseball history and it was made by a man who also hit 660 homers, stole 338 bases and batted .302 career. Players don't come more "complete" than that.

"I did a lot of things well because I enjoyed them all the same," Mays said. "I got as much of a thrill out of making a good play in the outfield as I did hitting a home run. I never broke the game down and said, 'OK, this is more important than this.' I did what I had to do to win the game, that's all.

"That's where I think young players today go wrong. They concentrate on doing this or doing that. I tell them, 'Hey, play the game. You've got to hit, run, and throw.' You've got guys 22 or 23 talking about being a DH. What kind of stuff is that?"

Ernie Banks played his first nine major league seasons at shortstop, the only 500 Clubber to make more than a token appearance in the middle infield. He spent his last 10 years at first base, a traditional power position, so younger fans might not realize what a remarkable all-around player Banks was.

The fact is, Banks won back-to-back National League MVP awards (1958 and '59) while playing shortstop for a losing team. (No player on a losing team ever had won the MVP award, much less two years in a row.) Banks also won a Gold Glove and set a league record with a .985 fielding percentage.

Mel Ott said Banks could have played shortstop on any team in any era. "How many shortstops could bat fourth in a lineup?" Ott asked. "I can think of Arky Vaughan, Glenn Wright, and maybe Travis Jackson. But this fellow [Banks] can do more things than any of them."

Mathews was regarded as the best third baseman of all-time before Schmidt came along. Even now, Mathews ranks as the No. 2 home run hitter at the position (with 481) behind only Schmidt, who passed him midway through last season.

Mathews wasn't much of a fielder when he signed with the Braves, but he learned fast under the direction of Billy Jurges, a former major league shortstop. Jurges taught Mathews to bend his knees, not bend from the waist, when reaching for a ground ball.

"You'd be amazed how many guys do it wrong," Mathews said. "You've got to see the ball before you can catch it. [Jurges] must have hit me 500 ground balls a day. It was a pain in the rear end but it paid off."

Mathews became a solid defensive player. In fact, he brought down the curtain on the Braves' lone World Series championship (1957) with a brilliant backhanded stop on the Yankees' Gil McDougald in Game 7.

Mathews also could run with the league's fastest players. As a rookie, he was timed from home to first in 3.5 seconds. Mathews could have stolen more bases but the way he was swinging the bat, his manager, Charlie Grimm, didn't want to risk an injury.

Mathews got off to the fastest start of anyone in the 500

circle. He hit 25 homers as a rookie, then led the National League with 47 his second year. The next two seasons Matthews hit 40 and 41.

That is 153 homers after just four years. Aaron, by comparison, had 110 home runs after his fourth season. Schmidt had 131. Babe Ruth still was a pitcher. Mathews seemed destined to break all the records.

Wrote the *Saturday Evening Post:* "This apple-cheeked third baseman has smashed epic clouts in every National League park. He stops traffic all over Milwaukee where the fans insist he will break the Babe's record."

Those expectations probably hurt Mathews in the long run as injuries and the daily grind of playing third base slowed him down. The fact that Aaron, a teammate, passed Mathews on his way to Ruth's record leaves, in Bill James's words, the feeling that Mathews was "a mild disappointment."

"I never looked at it that way," Mathews said, sipping a beer in the Braves' West Palm Beach, Fla., clubhouse. "The numbers never meant a damn thing to me. Other people set those goals. I just played hard every day and what happened happened.

"Yeah, I remember [the press] talking about me breaking Ruth's record. Even then I knew it was crazy. I had four seasons under my belt; I wasn't one-third of the way there. I'm happy as hell I made it to 500. How many guys have done it? I'd say I'm in pretty good company.

"I never thought of myself as a superstar," Mathews said. "I felt challenged every time I went on the field. Every series, I'd look at the other third baseman and think, 'I'm going to outplay you, you SOB.' We're talking about guys like Ken Boyer, Richie Allen, Jim Ray Hart. It wasn't easy.

"But I might have been a better competitor than I was a player. I loved the competition. It was a different game back then. They call Pete Rose 'Charlie Hustle.' Hell, we all played that way in the '50s and '60s. If you didn't play that way, they shipped you back to the Sally League."

Mathews was a fierce competitor, so was Frank Robinson. It was inevitable that in the 10 years they played against each other, their wills would collide in the vicinity of third base and shock waves would be felt across the National League. It happened in 1961 at Cincinnati.

Willie Mays wasn't there, but he knows the details well enough by now to provide a blow-by-blow description.

"Frank slid into Eddie real hard, the way he always did," Mays said. "Eddie told him not to do it again. Couple innings later, here comes Frank into third base even harder. Eddie got up swinging.

"Eddie gave it to Frank pretty good. Closed up one eye, left the other one like this [a slit]. The next day Frank was back in the lineup with both eyes swollen shut and he hit two home runs. Fred Haney [Milwaukee manager] gave Mathews hell for riling Frank up."

"A true story?" a visitor asked Mathews.

He took a slow drag on his cigarette. "Yeah, basically," he said.

Robinson's toughness is legend among players of that era. He had many great seasons—including a Triple Crown with Baltimore in 1966—but his Oriole teammates were more awed by the season he kept playing despite double vision (1968). Robinson was struck in the head by a throw while breaking up a doubleplay.

Fearless? Robinson stood with his toes almost touching home plate. His head and elbows dangled in the strike zone. National League pitchers drilled him 118 times in 10 seasons.

Don Drysdale knocked Robinson down four times in one game. Robinson got up and beat Drysdale with a grand slam in the final at-bat.

"I had a standing rule: Any of my pitchers who knocked Robinson down got a fine," Gene Mauch said. "He was dangerous at any time, but he was deadly when he was pissed off."

"Frank was the finest leader I've ever seen in this game," Elrod Hendricks said. "Rarely did he lead with words. It was usually by example.

"One night in Boston, Frank jammed his shoulder crashing into the fence on a ball hit by Reggie Smith. He had to bat the next inning but he couldn't take a full cut. So he dropped a bunt and brought in the tying run anyway.

"George Scott was playing third base. You should have

seen his face. He couldn't believe it: Frank Robinson bunting with a man on third. But we needed to get the run in and Frank did it the only way he could."

There is no telling how good Mantle could have been if he didn't have so many physical problems. Without question, the Mick's ratio of winces per homer is tops among 500 Clubbers.

A look at Mantle's medical file shows two operations on his right knee, one operation on his left knee, surgery on his right hip and shoulder, a broken foot, four broken fingers, six pulled hamstrings, and more groin and thigh tears than the Yankee trainers could possibly count.

He played his last 10 seasons with both legs wrapped in elastic bandages. It is said the constant pain and the fear of further injury was what soured Mantle's disposition. In that context, his surliness is more understandable.

"Mantle was not brittle, not really," said Dr. Sidney Gaynor, the team physician. "It was the demands he placed on himself: the stopping, the starting, the turning.

"It's truly remarkable that he could play 18 years on his legs. It took a remarkable amount of determination for him to do it. He never complained about the pain unless he was trying to help you make a diagnosis. He'd say, 'It hurts here,' and that would be it.

"The best description I'd give Mantle is he's the kind of guy you'd like to have in your outfit in a war."

Mantle was forced to retire at 37 after 18 major league seasons. He went out with 536 homers but folks kept saying, "What if . . ." The Mick passed the 400 mark at 31 and looked like a cinch for 600. Even the Babe's record wasn't out of the question.

"It wasn't meant to be," Mantle said. The passage of time has left him more philosophical than bitter.

"It wasn't a tough decision [to quit]. It was obvious I couldn't do the job anymore. I didn't hit worth a damn my last year [.237] and our team wasn't very good. I was walked an average of once every four at-bats.

"It was more frustrating than anything else. People ask if I feel cheated. I really don't. I had a lot of great years, I loved being a Yankee. I had an 18-year career. I never figured I'd last that long."

The best player of all-time? Bill James votes for Babe Ruth and it is hard to argue. It is common knowledge that Ruth began his major league career as a pitcher, but he wasn't just any pitcher. He was 23-12 in 1916 with nine shutouts (league high) and a 1.75 ERA. He was 24-13 the following year with 35 complete games (also a league high).

The Babe threw 24 consecutive shutout World Series innings, a record that stood for almost a half-century before the Yanks' Whitey Ford finally broke it in 1961.

So switching Ruth to the outfield was a move not unlike, say, the Red Sox putting Roger Clemens at third base.

Ruth was known for his power—he won a dozen American League home run titles—but he also hit for a .342 career average.

The Babe batted .356 in 1927, the year he hit 60 home runs. Roger Maris hit .269 the year he broke Ruth's record, 1961.

Ruth was not the blubbery lummox that revisionist authors made him out to be. He was a fine defensive outfielder who had 20 or more assists in two different seasons. (In 1986, Glenn Wilson and Toronto's Jesse Barfield tied for the major league lead with 20 outfield assists.)

Bill James rated Ruth with Frankie Frisch as the most aggressive baserunners of the '20s. Yes, the Babe could run. In 1921, Ruth had 44 doubles and 16 triples to go along with his 59 homers. (Last year, Juan Samuel had 36 doubles and 12 triples.)

Simply put: The Babe could hit for power and average, throw strikes from rightfield and the pitcher's mound, handle a glove and run the bases as well as anyone in his era.

He wasn't the most disciplined athlete around, but as the Babe himself pointed out: "We ain't playing in no Sunday school league." He seldom let his carousing interfere with his career, however. He loved the game too much for that.

The best pure hitter ever probably was Ted Williams. James agrees on that. So does Mauch, who was a utility infielder with Boston in 1957, the year Williams won his fifth American League batting title.

"Ted was the perfect hitting machine," Mauch said. "Great eyes, quick hands, strength and intelligence. He knew every inch of the strike zone.

"You give him the 2,000 at-bats Uncle Sam took away [Williams missed parts of five seasons due to military service] and you'd see numbers that might be unmatched by anybody. He would have had 600 homers for sure, maybe 700.

"Ted was so confident in his ability that if he faced a pitcher for the first time, he'd usually take two strikes just to see what the guy had. He'd say, 'OK, that's his fast-ball ... That's his curve ... Fine, now I've got him.' One swing was all Ted needed."

Confidence describes Williams as well as anything. When he joined the Sox in 1938, teammate Bobby Doerr told him: "Wait until you see this [Jimmie] Foxx hit."

Williams shot back, "Wait until Foxx sees me hit."

Doerr, the Sox captain, walked away shaking his head. It took awhile before the other players got used to Williams. A few never got used to him at all.

Williams liked to bring his bat back to the hotel after games and study his stance in the mirror. Once Williams was taking his cuts when he accidentally hit the bedpost and knocked the whole thing to pieces.

His roommate, Charley Wagner, heard the crash and came running out of the bathroom to find the mattress and box spring on the floor. Williams viewed the wreckage with typical detachment.

"Geez," Williams said. "What power."

Maybe that is how Williams got his nickname, the Splendid Splinter. The history books are unclear on that. But they are specific on the matter of Williams's eyesight: It was extraordinary and no doubt contributed to his ability to put his bat on a pitched ball.

When Williams went into the Marines, the doctors determined his eyesight was so keen, it might be found once in 100,000 men. At flight school, Williams broke the student gunnery record one week, then broke his own record the next.

As a hitter, he had no equal. He hit .406 in 1941 and no one has come close to touching that mark since. George Brett, Rod Carew and, Wade Boggs have flirted with it in recent years, but it is not likely to be done again in this era of the short reliever and the split-finger fastball.

It is interesting to note how the 500 Home Run Clubbers influenced each other and created their own little chain.

Williams, for example, had Babe Ruth's picture hanging in his bedroom. The Babe was Williams's idol. Mathews grew up copying the left-handed stance of Williams. And Schmidt chased after Mathews for an autograph when he was going to games at Crosley Field in Cincinnati.

Around and around it goes.

Who knows, maybe a future member of the 500 Club is waiting outside the Vet for Schmidt's autograph tonight. That is the cycle of baseball. And that is what keeps the game alive, for all of us.

HAMMERIN' HANK AND THE BABE

BY RAY DIDINGER

In the beginning, there is Aaron.

That is how the all-time player register in *The Baseball Encyclopedia* begins: Hank Aaron. Followed by his brother: Tommie Aaron. Followed by all the other guys who ever played the summer game.

It is ironic, and fitting, that baseball's alphabetical leadoff man should be first in so many ways: Total bases (6,856), extra base hits (1,477), RBI (2,297) and, of course, home runs (755).

Maybe God planned it that way.

"Then God should have made it easier," Hank Aaron said. "As it was, I went through H-E-L-L setting those records. I wish I could look back on it as a happy time but I can't. There was too much pain."

Aaron was seated behind his desk at the Atlanta Braves' spring training site in West Palm Beach, Fla. It is hard to believe, but Aaron is now 53 and in his 11th season as the club's director of player development.

It is 13 years since the Hammer turned on an Al Downing fastball and drove it 420 feet through the misty night at Atlanta Stadium. The 52,780 paying customers—and the millions who watched on TV—will never forget the moment the ball disappeared into the Braves' bullpen and into legend.

Fireworks lit up the sky. The scoreboard screamed "HANK" in letters 8-feet high. Aaron circled the bases flanked briefly by two teenagers who rushed onto the field. Somewhere along the way, Aaron lapped the ghost of George Herman Ruth.

That was home run No. 715, breaking the Babe's career mark that had stood for 39 years. Ruth had predicted someone would break his record of 60 homers in a season—Roger Maris did, in 1961—but the Babe thought his 714 total was safe forever.

Then along came Hank Aaron.

"I don't know quite how to put this," Aaron said, shifting his gaze out the window to the practice field. "Breaking the record was a tremendous experience, but it was also a letdown. It was nothing like I thought it would be.

"I thought if I hit 715, things would be a lot better in my life. Instead, they got worse. I got to the top of the mountain and there was nothing but hostility. I kept thinking, 'It's not supposed to be like this.' I came away not trusting people as much."

Aaron looked back at his visitor. "You asked me what I remember," he said. "Well, that's what I remember. It was a great honor, it was the highlight of my career, but it's still a bittersweet feeling.

"I had hoped it would be only sweet."

■

Hank Aaron has not forgotten the hate mail that poured in during that season, the taunts from those who could not accept a black man eclipsing a white hero.

Even in Atlanta, there were bumper stickers that read "Aaron is Ruthless." In San Francisco, a fan leaned into the dugout and hit the 40-year-old outfielder in the face with an orange.

Aaron had to travel under an assumed name that season. Partly, it was to find refuge from the media posse that followed him across the country. Partly, it was to protect him from the cranks who regularly phoned in death threats.

It was, as Dickens might have written, the best of times and the worst of times.

"If I was white, all America would be proud of me," Aaron said bitterly.

Aaron saw it as a purely racial issue, which is understandable perhaps but not entirely correct.

Maris, a white man, went through a similar ordeal the year he hit 61 home runs. He was jeered by the fans and much of his mail wasn't so nice, either. America simply did not want to see its one and only Babe taken down from the pedestal.

As columnist Chalmers Roberts wrote in The *Washington Post*:

"It is simply a matter of moorings. The Empire State Building may not be the world's tallest anymore, but it is for me. Most of us are captives of our memories. And that goes for me and George Herman Ruth, the Babe."

Roberts summed up by wishing Aaron luck but acknowledging if the Braves' slugger did succeed, "he [Aaron] would have knocked a great big hole in my nostalgia."

So the backlash Aaron felt might have been as much pro-Ruth as anti-Hank. And the majority of Americans *were* behind the Hammer. But the days leading up to the big event—April 8, 1974—were filled with little subplots that drained much of the joy:

- Commissioner Bowie Kuhn ordered Aaron to play two of the first three games in Cincinnati. Aaron was one homer shy of the record and there was talk the Braves might sit him out until they returned to Atlanta to assure a big gate.
- Cincinnati management asked Aaron what it could do to honor him. Aaron suggested a moment of silence for Martin Luther King since it was April 4, the anniversary of King's death.

The Reds said sorry, they did not get involved in politics. That same day, Vice President Gerald Ford threw out the first ball at Riverfront Stadium. "That really stuck in my craw," Aaron said.

- Aaron hit No. 714 on the first pitch thrown to him by the Reds' Jack Billingham. He didn't get another hit in the series and went down on three weak swings in his final at-bat against Clay Kirby. A few writers suggested Aaron went in the tank to save No. 715 for the home crowd.

"I've never gone on the field and not given my level best," Aaron said. "It makes me furious that anyone would say that. Don't they think I have any pride?"

- The night Aaron broke the record, Kuhn was inexplicably attending a cocktail party in Cleveland. The commissioner sent an aide, Monte Irvin, to represent him. Aaron seethed over that for years.

In 1980, Aaron was to be honored in New York for the "outstanding baseball feat of the '70s." Kuhn was to make the presentation. Aaron refused to attend, pointing out Kuhn didn't see fit to show up the night the feat took place.

■ Also, sports writers insisted on making comparisons, pointing out Aaron had played more games than Ruth, gone to bat 2,000 more times, played in a ballpark they called "the launching pad" and so forth.

What they were saying, basically, is Aaron hit more homers but he still ain't the Babe. Aaron bristled at the comparisons: day games vs. night games; the "dead" ball vs. the "lively" ball; the eight-team league vs. expansion; etc.

"If a writer can't find something better than that to print, he's in sad shape," Aaron said. "They tried to make me sound like some rinky-dink. I'm No. 3 all-time in hits behind [Pete] Rose and [Ty] Cobb. I'm No. 2 [behind Cobb] in runs scored.

"I'll stack my numbers up against anybody. I was a productive player for over 20 years. You can talk all you want about ballparks and longer seasons . . . you've still got to step up there and hit the ball. There's no shortcut to 700 home runs.

"This might sound conceited, but I didn't feel there was a player in the league who was any better than me. Yet I was always mentioned behind Willie Mays, Mickey Mantle, and Frank Robinson. For years, I felt somewhat slighted by awards and things presented to other players.

"If I didn't hit 715, I would have never been recognized for the player I was. Even when I did it, there were people who wouldn't give me my due. It used to bother me but not anymore. The numbers are there. Anybody who knows baseball knows what they mean.

"The other people," Aaron said with a wave, "aren't worth worrying about."

■

Aaron never asked to be measured against the Babe. He was just hoping to play well enough to get by when he left his Mobile, Ala., home at 17 with $2 in his pocket and two sandwiches in a brown paper bag.

The year was 1951 and Aaron was signing on with the

Indianapolis Clowns, a barnstorming Black team. "We didn't have roommates," Aaron recalled, "we had seatmates. We ate and slept on the bus."

Aaron was discovered by Dewey Griggs, a scout for the Boston Braves. Griggs saw Aaron go 7-for-9 in a doubleheader with two home runs. The Braves bought his contract from the Clowns for $10,000. The team got the money; Aaron got nothing.

Aaron spent his first professional season in Eau Claire, Wis., where he hit .336 in Class C ball. In 1953, the Braves moved him to Class A. The only trouble was their Jacksonville, Fla., team played in the all-white Sally League. Aaron and teammate Felix Mantilla broke the color line.

It was a bitter time, with white folks tossing bottles from the stands. Even at home, there was silence when the two black players were introduced. Aaron carried those scars for a long while.

That is why Aaron now sees things in shades of black and white. That is why he says things like: "Ruth's record was considered the greatest until I broke it. Then Joe DiMaggio's record [56-game hitting streak] became the greatest. Isn't that funny?"

If that sounds cynical, Aaron says, so be it. And if people squirm when he says there aren't enough blacks in major league front offices, fine. Let them start counting. They will see he is right.

"I talked about these things for years but nobody listened until I started closing in on 714," Aaron said. "Writers asked, 'Why weren't you saying all this before?' I said, 'I was. Why weren't you paying attention?'

"That was one of the worst things about that year. I was misquoted so many times. I tried to get along with the press my whole career, but it got nasty in 1974 because things were printed out of context. Finally, I got fed up with it."

The irony is Aaron spent most of his career complaining he was lost in the sticks while Mays and Mantle enjoyed the media spotlight in New York. When the attention finally came Aaron's way, it was a global avalanche that almost buried him.

Aaron was not a colorful figure and, in truth, would not

have generated much publicity in New York or anywhere else if it were not for his run at the Babe. Aaron didn't have the on-stage flair of Mays nor did he see the need to cultivate it.

Aaron was a ballplayer, period.

"People said I wasn't exciting," Aaron said. "What's exciting? What were they looking for?

"How exciting was Joe DiMaggio? He was a good player but he didn't hit any tape-measure homers. How about Ted Williams? He didn't steal many bases. Didn't knock himself out on defense, either. How exciting was he?

"What's exciting? I could have worn a size 7 cap instead of 7½, that way it would have fallen off my head everytime I ran the bases [a jab at Mays' trademark]. I could have hit the dirt every time a pitch came close to me.

"But I wanted to play the game my way. I felt the bottom line was production. The only excitement I cared about was winning. So I'd hit 40 home runs in a season and read about a guy who hit 25 and was called a superstar. I guess I was taken for granted after a while."

The man Aaron pursued through baseball's time capsule, of course, was the most colorful player ever. The Babe. The Bambino. The Sultan of Swat. The Maharajah of Mash. Ruth brought the game back from the Black Sox scandal on the strength of his personality and talent.

In 1920, his first year with the Yankees, Ruth hit 54 home runs. That was more than any other American League *team* that season. The Babe revolutionized the game with his power and captured the nation's imagination with his off-the-field antics.

Writes Bill James in his *Baseball Abstract:* "Like Napoleon, Babe Ruth was a remarkable man who came along at one of the gates of history when the old ways had been destroyed and men were anxious to be shown the way to a safe new place."

Ruth won the home run championship 10 times in 12 years. He hit over 50 homers in four different seasons. Due largely to the Babe's drawing power, American League attendance went from 1.7 million in 1918 to 5 million in 1920.

"[Ruth] was the most famous person in the country during the 1920s," wrote Robert Creamer in The *New York Times*.

"Jack Dempsey, Charlie Chaplin, Charles Lindbergh, and possibly Calvin Coolidge were as well known by name as Ruth, but not so well known in public.

"Ruth dominated his team, his league, his sport, his environment. Wherever Babe Ruth was, he was the center of attention."

Aaron was no match for Ruth in the charisma department. Where the Babe was larger than life, Aaron actually seemed smaller than his 6-feet, 180 pounds.

When Aaron met President Nixon at the 1969 All-Star game, he offered a polite, "Hello, Mr. President," When the Babe met President Warren Harding on a warm summer day, he observed, "Hot as hell, ain't it, Prez?"

Different strokes, indeed.

Claire Ruth, the Babe's widow, claimed her late husband would have rooted for Aaron to break his record. Other people close to the Babe aren't so sure. They said he was very protective of his legacy.

■

The Hammer shows the signs of middle age. His face is round. His stomach sags over his belt. Even in spring training, his front office duties keep Aaron bound to his desk most of the day.

He enjoys his work, overseeing Atlanta's minor league system. The six farm teams were a collective 57 games over .500 in 1986, which means Aaron's 60-hour weeks are paying off. There is a lot of good young talent ripening in Aaron's vineyard.

"I'm content," he said. "This is the lifeblood of your organization. This is where it all begins. If you don't get quality here, you don't get it later. I like this role: finding good kids and bringing them along.

"I like it better than coaching at the major league level. I can't imagine offering help to some .220 hitter and having him reject me. That would be hard for me to accept but that's how those guys are. At least the kids will listen when you talk to them.

"I just had two in here this morning," Aaron said. "I told them they have the talent but they lack that mental edge.

Sometimes it's a matter of growing up. After all, they are just kids. But they have to show they want it.

"I tell them what's expected, what we're thinking and where they stand. After that it's up to them. Every kid in this camp did something to excite our scouts. That's how they got here. Now we have to find out who can compete at this level.

"The game is changing and not for the better. Every rookie who comes along wants to have a good season and sign a $10 million contract. You have veterans like Bob Hoerner and Tim Raines who priced themselves out of the league.

"That's why I don't think you'll see anyone break my home run record. The top players won't hang around 23 years, which is what it will take. They will get so rich in 12 years, they will just quit. You won't see the Roses and Niekros anymore."

Aaron wanted to hang around because he knew what was waiting back in Mobile, Ala. He didn't want to wind up in the shipyard with his father, pulling down $75 a week. So he worked on his hitting until his callouses felt like stucco.

"I had a God-given talent," Aaron said, "but I studied the fine points of hitting. I remember the first spring training with the Braves. We toured with the Dodgers.

"They had Newcombe, Erskine, Podres, Labine. Podres had one of the best changeups and curveballs around. I'd come out of the Sally League, which was nothing but fastballs.

"I got off to a good start but wherever we went, the papers said: 'Wait until the season starts. We'll see if the skinny kid from Jacksonville can hit.' It was frightening.

"We went through Chattanooga and Nashville and they had me looking ridiculous with the off-speed stuff. Charlie Grimm [the manager] said, 'Don't worry about it, kid.'

"As time came along, I became a better breaking ball hitter than a fastball hitter. Nine out of 10 pitchers, if they make a mistake, they make it with the breaking ball.

"Anyway, that winter I went home. My brother and I and the other kids went to the ballpark and I worked on it. I said, 'I'm either going to be a major league player or they're going to run me out of the league.' "

Aaron lasted 23 years, the final two as a designated hitter

with the Milwaukee Brewers. On his last visit to Oakland, Aaron ripped a line drive into the centerfield bleachers, 430 feet away. The ball struck a fan in the head and knocked him off his feet and back into his seat.

"I hit it good," Aaron said later.

That was homer No. 750. Five more followed, his last one coming against California's Dick Drago on July 20, 1976. And so ended an era, but not a legend.

Hank Aaron. The first words in the player register. The last words on home runs.

500 CLUB PROFILES

COMPILED BY RAY DIDINGER

Hank Aaron

Position: Outfielder
Height, Weight: 6-foot, 180
Batted: Right
Born: Feb. 5, 1934 in Mobile, Ala.
Currently: Director of player development for the Atlanta Braves.

Background: Aaron was the third of eight children. His father worked as a boilermaker's helper in the Alabama shipyard. As a youth, Aaron idolized Jackie Robinson and sharpened his batting eye by hitting bottle caps with a broom handle.

A star athlete in high school, Aaron left home at 17 to join the Indianapolis Clowns, a barnstorming black team. A Boston Braves scout spotted Aaron, then a shortstop, and purchased his contract for $10,000.

He was in the major leagues two years later. Aaron became a starting outfielder his rookie year in Milwaukee (1954) when veteran Bobby Thomson broke his ankle during spring training. The rest is history.

Career Highlights: Aaron holds the all-time major league record for home runs, total bases (6,856), extra base hits (1,477) and RBI (2,297). He also appeared in a record 24 All-Star games.

Aaron won National League MVP Award in 1957. A fine all-around player, Aaron won three Gold Gloves (1958-60) and was successful on 143 of 170 stolen base attempts (84 percent) from 1963-68. He won the National League batting championship twice and home run title four times.

Aaron retired in 1976 with a .305 career average. He hit .364 (20-for-55) in two World Series appearances. He was voted into the Hall of Fame in 1982.

No. 500: Aaron hit his 500th home run off the Giants' Mike McCormick on July 14, 1968. He was 34 at the time and playing in his 15th major league season.

Etcetera: Aaron did not have his own bat his first year in the majors. He just grabbed any old bat off the rack when it was his turn to hit. Manager Birdie Tebbetts convinced Aaron it might be a good idea to order a few bats of his own.

Also, the night Aaron hit his 715th home run to pass Babe Ruth, he was wearing a pair of baseball shoes discarded by ex-Yankee and ex-Brave Joe Pepitone.

Other Views: Bobby Thomson, teammate: "Magic is the only way to describe [Aaron]. You had this feeling even then [1954] that this guy was something special. He was far removed from the ordinary class of ballplayer like the rest of us."

Tommy Davis, opponent: "All I know about [Aaron] is he waits on the pitched ball better than anyone I ever saw, moves any kind of pitch in more directions than any of us and is the best man in the world with a bat. The players call him 'Wrists' or 'The Most.' "

Babe Ruth

Position: Outfielder
Height, Weight: 6-2, 215
Batted: Left
Born: Feb. 6, 1895 in Baltimore, Md.
Died: Aug. 16, 1948 in New York
Background: Ruth was the son of a Baltimore saloon-keeper. At age 8, he was packed off to St. Mary's, a combination orphanage and reform school. He lived there until he was 19 when he signed with the Baltimore Orioles, then a minor league team.

Ruth was in the majors with Boston in less than one year.

He was a pitcher with the Red Sox and he won 65 games in three seasons (1915-17). He threw nine shutouts in 1916, an American League record for lefthanders that stood for 62 years until the Yanks' Ron Guidry tied it in 1978.

In 1920, Boston owner Harry Frazee sold Ruth to the Yankees for $125,000. Frazee was a theatrical producer who needed the money to cover his debts. The deal made the Yankees and made baseball. Ruth became the No. 1 personality in American sports.

Career Highlights: Ruth moved to the outfield in New York and won 10 home run titles in 12 years. He compiled a .342 career batting average, 11th best all-time. His slugging percentage (.690) leads all players.

In 1927, Ruth hit 32 of his record 60 home runs on the road. He also hit 17 off lefthanded pitching. Ruth averaged one homer in every 11.8 times at-bat, the highest ratio ever. (Aaron averaged one in every 16.4 at-bats.)

Most amazing thing about Ruth was his consistency. He hit 41 or more home runs in nine of 10 seasons (1923-32). The only year he missed was 1925 when he was out two months with an abdominal abscess.

No. 500: Ruth hit his 500th off Cleveland's Willis Hundlin on Aug. 11, 1929. He was 34 and in his 16th season.

Etcetera: To give you an idea how Ruth dwarfed his peers, baseball's career home run leader before Ruth was Roger Connor with 136. The Babe passed him in his first full season with the Yankees.

Also, Ruth's 60 home runs in 1927 was more than any other American League *team* that season. In fact, it was more than Cleveland and Boston combined (54). The Babe also hit more homers than any AL team in 1920 with 54.

Other Views: Dick Schaap, author: "Babe Ruth remains the personification of professional sports in America . . . He was living proof, and is still mythic proof, that through sports a man can rise from common, vulgar beginnings to wealth, to fame, to a position of influence attained only by movie stars and singers and a handful of presidents."

Willie Mays

Position: Outfielder
Height, Weight: 5-11, 170
Batted: Right
Born: May 6, 1931 in Westfield, Ala.
Currently: Special assistant to the president of the San Francisco Giants.

Background: Mays grew up poor on the outskirts of Birmingham, Ala. His father, Willie Sr., was a semi-pro outfielder. His grandfather, Walter, was a sandlot pitcher of note in Tuscaloosa.

Mays was a superb, all-around athlete in high school. He felt football, not baseball, would be his best sport. But colleges weren't recruiting black quarterbacks in the '40s. Mays opted to sign with the Birmingham Black Barons, a Negro League team.

The Giants signed Mays to a contract and brought him to the majors in 1951 at age 20. He spent the next two seasons in the Army, then returned to win the National League batting title (.345) and MVP Award en route to the 1954 World Series.

It was during that series Mays made his famous over-the-shoulder catch against Cleveland's Vic Wertz.

Career Highlights: Many experts, including former Giants manager Leo Durocher, point to Mays as the finest all-around ballplayer who ever lived. Says Gene Mauch: "Mays could beat you more ways than anybody."

Mays won 12 Gold Gloves in consecutive seasons (1956-68) and stole 338 bases in his career. He led the National League in home runs four times and stolen bases four times, a rare combination.

Mays's home run output was hampered by playing in Candlestick Park, where the wind usually blew in from leftfield. Mays feels he could have hit more than 700 homers if he played those 14 years in another ballpark.

No. 500: Mays hit his 500th home run off the Astro's Don Nottebart on Sept. 13, 1965. Mays, 34, reached the milestone in his 14th season, faster than any other player.

Etcetera: Mays claims his most memorable home run was the one he hit in his first game as a Met (May 14, 1972). He hit it against the Giants, who had traded the fading 41-year-old star to New York just two days earlier. "All the [Giants] players shook my hand as I rounded the bases," Mays said. "When I came around third, I looked in their dugout and they were giving me a standing ovation. My knees were shaking so much, I wasn't sure I'd be able to make it home.

"But I did."

Other Views: Willie McCovey, teammate: "I don't see how anyone could have been better than Mays. He was head and shoulders above everybody else."

Monte Irvin, teammate: "Willie's territory in the Polo Grounds was from second base to the centerfield monument. Nobody could cover that fairway the way Willie could."

Frank Robinson

Position: Outfielder
Height, Weight: 6-1, 183
Batted: Right
Born: Aug. 31, 1935 in Beaumont, Texas.
Currently: Coach with the Baltimore Orioles.
Background: Robinson was the youngest of 10 children. His father was a railway brakeman. The family moved to Oakland when Robinson was 5 and that is where he grew up.

He was a star outfielder on the Oakland American Legion all-star team that won the national title in 1950. Fourteen kids off that squad signed pro contracts but only Robinson and catcher J.W. Porter made it to the majors.

Robinson played 10 seasons with Cincinnati, then was traded before the 1966 season to Baltimore for pitchers Milt Pappas, Jack Baldschun, and infielder Dick Simpson. Reds general manager Bill DeWitt explained, "Robinson is an old 30." Robinson went on to win the Triple Crown that year.

Career Highlights: Robinson is the only man to be named Most Valuable Player in both leagues (Cincinnati,

1961, and Baltimore, 1966). He also was National League Rookie of the Year (1956) and a gold Glove winner (1958).

A 1963 survey of National League players by *Sport* magazine rated Robinson the No. 1 rightfielder ahead of Aaron and Roberto Clemente. Bill James rated Robinson the most aggressive baserunner of the '60s.

In 1975, Robinson became baseball's first black manager when he was named player-manager in Cleveland. He had the Indians over .500 in his second year but he was fired in 1977. Robinson managed the San Francisco Giants to a third-place finish in 1982.

No. 500: Robinson hit his 500th off Detroit's Fred Scherman on Sept. 13, 1971. He was 36 and in his 16th season.

Etcetera: Robinson was a fierce competitor, even in exhibitions. In 1976, the Indians met their Toledo farm team in a charity game. The Toledo pitcher, Bob Reynolds, threw a ball over Robinson's head.

Reynolds, it seems, still was annoyed at Robinson, the player-manager, for sending him to the minors. Words were exchanged as Robinson walked toward first base. Pretty soon, they were trading punches.

Did Robinson regret it later? "If the circumstances were the same," he said, "I'd do it again."

Other Views: Birdie Tebbetts, former Reds manager: "Frank has wonderful bat control. He has complete control of the muscles in his arms and wrists."

Sparky Anderson, Tigers manager: "There are some ballplayers that if you can get 'em mad, they can't do a thing. Other players will fight you tooth and nail; they'll kill you. Frank Robinson is that way."

Harmon Killebrew

Position: First Baseman, Third Baseman, Outfield
Height, Weight: 6-foot, 195
Batted: Right
Born: June 29, 1936 in Payette, Idaho.
Currently: Broadcaster for the Minnesota Twins.
Background: Killebrew came by his strength naturally.

His father was a star fullback at West Virginia Wesleyan. His grandfather, the original Harmon Clayton Killebrew, was reputed to be heavyweight wrestling champion of the Union Army during the Civil War.

Young Harmon turned down a football scholarship to Oregon to sign a $50,000 bonus contract with the Washington Senators in 1954. The Senators found Killebrew through a tip by a real senator, Democrat Herman Welker, of Idaho, who knew the family.

The bonus rule was in effect, which meant the Senators had to keep the 18-year-old Killebrew on their major league roster for at least two years. He played sparingly (113 at-bats) but learned a lot.

Career Highlights: Killebrew is second only to Babe Ruth among all-time American League home run hitters. He averaged one home run in every 14.22 at-bats, third behind Ruth and Ralph Kiner.

The Killer, as he was called, won or shared the American League home run title six times and belted more than 40 homers in eight seasons. He was voted the league's Most Valuable Player in 1969.

He played three different positions—first base, third base, outfield—in his 22-year career. Baseball historian Bill James rates Killebrew as the game's No. 2 all-time multi-position player, behind Pete Rose.

No. 500: Killebrew hit his 500th off Baltimore's Mike Cuellar on Aug. 10, 1971. He was 35 and playing in his 18th season.

Etcetera: Following up on No. 500: Killebrew struggled mightily to reach that milestone. He was stuck on No. 499 for almost a month. He admits the pressure got to him.

"The Twins had these plastic cups made up to commemorate the 500th," Killebrew said, "and they just sat around for a month. It was getting embarrassing . . . When I finally hit it, I felt like a weight was lifted off my shoulders."

Other Views: President Dwight Eisenhower: "I don't follow baseball all that closely, but my grandson David does and this Killebrew fellow is his greatest hero. That's why I wanted to stop by and shake his hand."

Reggie Jackson

Position: Outfielder
Height, Weight: 6-foot, 195
Bats: Left
Born: May 18, 1946 in Wyncote, Pa.
Currently: Designated hitter with Oakland.

Background: Jackson was the sixth in a family of seven children. His mother and father divorced and Reggie was raised in the Philadelphia suburbs by his father, Martinez Jackson, a tailor.

Reggie was a three-sport star at Cheltenham High School and won a scholarship to Arizona State. He played baseball and football (halfback under Frank Kush) for the Sun Devils but left after two years when he was drafted by the Kansas City A's.

The New York Mets had the first pick overall in that 1966 draft, but they passed over Jackson to select catcher Steve Chilcott, of Lancaster, Calif. Chilcott never played an inning in the majors. The A's took Jackson with the No. 2 pick.

Career Highlights: "Mr. October" surely will go down as one of baseball's most colorful figures. Jackson began this season as the all-time leader with 2,500 strikeouts. That is an average of one whiff in every 3.8 at-bats.

His career batting average (.263) won't win any awards but he has hit 20 or more home runs 16 times, tying an American League record. He was the league's Most Valuable Player in 1973 (32 homers, 117 RBI).

Jackson's finest hour came in Game 6 of the 1977 World Series when he hit three consecutive homers to lead the Yankees to the championship. His five home runs in the series was a record.

No. 500: Jackson hit his 500th off the Royals' Bud Black on Sept. 17, 1984. He was 38 and playing in his 17th season.

Etcetera: At his peak, Jackson was perhaps the best physical specimen among the 500 Clubbers. He had a 34-inch waist, 27-inch thighs, and 17-inch biceps. He was timed in 9.7 seconds for 100 yards.

Also, Jackson credits ex-Phillie Dick Allen for telling him to use a heavier bat. Allen said a heavy bat (Jackson went from 34 ounces to 36) would force him to make his hands quicker.

Other Views: Don Sutton, former teammate: "Reggie is a charlatan but a charlatan with credentials. He cons people and sells himself, but he produces."

Thomas Boswell, *Washington Post* sports writer: "Jackson can mix hokum and genuine insight, subtle phrasing and pathetic bombast like no other star. Few men can match his knack for having a good idea, then mopping the floor with it."

Mickey Mantle

Position: Outfielder
Height, Weight: 5-11, 195
Batted: Both
Born: Oct. 20, 1931 in Spavinaw, Okla.
Currently: Broadcaster on New York's SportsChannel Network.

Background: Mantle was one of five children born to a semi-pro ballplayer (his father) and a former high school track champion (his mother). Mickey inherited their athletic abilities but injuries haunted him from the start.

Doctors discovered osteomyelitis, an infectious inflammatory disease of the bone marrow, in Mantle's leg when he was in high school. He kept playing despite the pain and signed with the Yankees' Independence (Kan.) farm team in 1949. His bonus: a modest $1,150.

Mantle made it to the majors in 1951 and suffered his first serious knee injury, stepping on a sprinkler in the Yankee Stadium outfield. That led to the first of three knee operations in Mantle's 18-year career.

Career Highlights: Bill James puts Mantle, at his peak, as the No. 1 centerfielder of all-time, ahead of Ty Cobb, Mays, and Joe DiMaggio.

Mantle won the Triple Crown in 1956, batting .353 with 52 homers and 130 RBI. He picked up the first of his three American League MVP Awards the same year. He finished second in the voting three other times.

Mantle is the most prolific hitter in World Series history

with 18 homers and 40 RBI. He popularized the "tape-measure" homer. His all-time monster was a 565-foot blast that hit a tenement house next to Griffith Stadium in Washington.

No. 500: Mantle hit his 500th off Baltimore's Stu Miller on May 14, 1967. He was 35 and in his 17th season. The Mick was in a 4-for-33 slump before the homer.

Etcetera: In 1961, Roger Maris broke Ruth's record with 61 home runs but he barely nosed out Mantle for the MVP Award. (Maris won by four votes.) Mantle had a great year, batting .317 with 54 homers (a career high) and 128 RBI.

Also, Mantle might have been the toughest man in major league history to double. He hit into just 113 career doubleplays, that's one in every 71.7 at-bats.

Other Views: Bill James, baseball historian: "Mickey Mantle was, at his peak in 1956-57 and again in 1961-62, clearly a greater player than Willie Mays and it is not a close or difficult decision."

Jimmie Foxx

Position: First Baseman
Height, Weight: 6-foot, 195
Batted: Right
Born: Oct. 22, 1907 in Sudlersville, Md.
Died: July 21, 1967 in Miami.

Background: Foxx grew up on the family farm, doing a man's work when he was 12 years old. He developed his powerful upper body by loading and unloading the large milk cans on the truck.

He started playing ball in his teens, signing with the Easton (Del.) team in the Class D Eastern Shore League. Connie Mack signed Foxx for the A's as an 18-year-old catcher in 1925. He blossomed later at first base.

A *Philadelphia Bulletin* story described Foxx as: "a naturally bright and up-and-doing young country boy with plenty of confidence, a desire to get on and having the strength of an ox."

Career Highlights: Foxx was one of baseball's top sluggers in the '30s. He had 58 homers and had two others washed out by rain in the 1932 season. With better luck, he could have tied Ruth's record of 60.

Foxx won the American League's MVP Award three times (1932-33-38) in an era when Ruth, Lou Gehrig, and Al Simmons, among others, were around. He hit 30 or more homers a record 12 years in a row (1929-40).

Foxx won two batting titles, four home run titles and a Triple Crown in 1933 (.356, 48, 163). He had a .344 average in three World Series with the A's. Foxx was one of the first men to hit a ball over the leftfield roof in Comiskey Park.

No. 500: Foxx hit his 500th off the A's George Caster on Sept. 24, 1940. He was 32 (youngest ever) and in his 16th season.

Etcetera: Foxx was nicknamed "the Beast" because of his powerful physique and long-distance home runs. In his first season in Boston, Foxx hit a ball over the centerfield wall (450 feet) in Fenway Park.

In Ted Williams's book, *My Turn at Bat*, Williams claims Foxx regularly carried a flask of Scotch in his hip pocket. Foxx floundered after he left baseball in the '40s and went broke due to poor investments.

Other Views: Bill James: "If Jimmie Foxx were growing up today, he would probably end up as an NFL linebacker. A man of enormous upper-body strength, Foxx was light on his feet and had a fearsome throwing arm.

"His best seasons are quite comparable to Gehrig's or even Ruth's, and it is only by careful analysis that one can be sure that he was not, indeed, the greatest first baseman who ever lived."

Ted Williams

Position: Outfielder
Height, Weight: 6-3, 205
Batted: Left
Born: Aug. 30, 1918 in San Diego.
Currently: Sports and fitness consultant to Sears, Roebuck and Co.
Background: Williams was raised by his mother, a Salvation Army worker "whose will," wrote John Chamber-

lain in *Life* magazine, "is almost as imperious as that of her son."

She did not approve of her son playing baseball for a living, but Williams had his own ideas. He signed with the San Diego Padres (a minor league team) right out of high school and displayed an immediate genius with the bat.

He hit .327 as a Red Sox rookie in 1939 with 31 homers and 145 RBI, tops in the league. There is no telling what kind of numbers Williams might have compiled if he had not missed all or parts of five seasons due to military service.

Career Highlights: Williams's statistics become more dazzling with the passage of time. He was the last .400 hitter we are likely to see. He hit .406 (with 37 homers) in 1941 to win the first of six American League batting crowns.

Williams won back-to-back batting titles in 1957-58, the last one at age 40.

Williams's career batting average is .344, sixth best in baseball history. He was famous for his patience at the plate. Williams had 2,019 walks in his 19-year career, second only to Ruth. He had, in fact, almost three times as many walks as strikeouts (709). Amazing.

No. 500: Williams hit his 500th off Cleveland's Wynn Hawkins on June 17, 1960. He was 41 (the oldest ever) and in his 19th season.

Etcetera: During the Korean conflict, Williams flew in the same fighter squadron as John Glenn, the astronaut-turned-politican. Williams must have had The Right Stuff, too, because he outscored Glenn (and everyone else) in gunnery school.

During one raid, Williams's Panther jet was hit by enemy ground fire. His radio failed, his airspeed indicator was gone and his engine was on fire. He nursed the plane back to base, executed a successful belly landing and emerged without a scratch.

Other Views: John Chamberlain: "Ted derives his power from the extra flick delivered at the last second by sinewy wrists and great forearms. Ted's bat moves wickedly through the air with a long, silky swish that makes one think of a snake uncoiling or a Russian wolfhound bounding over a hedge."

Thomas Boswell: "Williams was a one-man drama larger than most of the games the Red Sox played. He dominated the scene, separated himself from his teammates and made no bones about being a prima donna. When he walked to the batting cage, the seas parted, he took his cuts and left when he was good and ready."

Willie McCovey

Position: First Baseman
Height, Weight: 6-4, 198
Batted: Left
Born: Jan. 10, 1938 in Mobile, Ala.
Currently: Special assistant to the president of the San Francisco Giants.

Background: McCovey was the seventh of 10 children born to church-going Baptist parents. In fact, his parents forbade the teenaged Willie to play baseball on Sunday because they considered it a sin.

McCovey grew to his full height by age 16, which made him a three-sport star at Central High in Mobile. He tried to enlist in the Navy at 16 but his mother stopped him.

He worked part-time in a produce market and played baseball at night. He was discovered by a scout, Jesse Thomas, who signed him for the Giants. He spent four years in the minors before joining the giants in 1959.

Career Highlights: McCovey had an auspicious major league debut. Called up from the Pacific Coast League on July 29, McCovey was rushed into the lineup against the Phillies' Robin Roberts. He went 4-for-4 (two singles, two triples).

McCovey never did cool off that season. He finished with a .354 average for 52 games and won the National League's Rookie of the Year Award. He slumped to .238 the next year, however, and that was typical of his up-and-down career.

McCovey won the MVP Award in 1969 (.320, 45, 126) and led the league in homers three times. He was Comeback Player of the Year with the Giants in 1977 when he hit .280 with 28 homers. He was dropped by two teams—San Diego and Oakland—the previous season.

No. 500: McCovey hit his 500th off Atlanta's Jamie Easterly on June 30, 1978. He was 40 and in his 20th season.

Etcetera: McCovey tore cartilage in his knee in 1971 and played the whole season on it, taking pain-killer shots rather than surgery that would have sidelined him.

As a result, McCovey had a gimpy leg the rest of his career. He also missed half the 1972 season with a broken arm. But he worked hard to keep his body in shape. That is how he played into his 40s.

Other Views: Al Jackson, former Mets pitcher: "Willie had a few holes in his strike zone . . . areas you could get him out, especially if you were a lefty [pitcher]. But he got smarter as he got older and he got a lot more selective at the plate. And if you made a mistake, Lord, could he make you pay."

Jessie Thomas, scout: "When I put Willie on the bus [for the Giants' camp], I gave him a dollar for hot dogs and stuff and told him if he came back home, I wanted my dollar back."

Eddie Mathews

Position: Third baseman
Height, Weight: 6-1, 190
Batted: Left
Born: Oct. 13, 1931 in Texarkana, Texas.
Currently: Minor league hitting instructor for the Atlanta Braves.

Background: Mathews was first exposed to professional baseball by his father, a Western Union wire chief in Santa Barbara who covered the local California State League for years.

Mathews was a gifted athlete in high school, an all-state halfback who had his pick of college scholarship offers. He chose to sign with the Boston Braves for $6,000 because his family needed the money. His father was stricken with tuberculosis.

Mathews was an immediate sensation in the Class A Southern Association. He hit five tape-measure home runs, including a 500-foot blast into a magnolia tree in Atlanta. He also cleared a 30-foot wall 420 feet from home plate in Chattanooga.

Career Highlights: Mathews got off to the fastest start of anyone in the 500 Club, hitting 153 homers in his first four major league seasons. He led the National League with 47 homers in his second year, 1953.

Although his pace slowed, Mathews remained a productive player through 13 seasons in Milwaukee. He won a second home run title in 1959 (46), batted over .300 three times and led the league in walks four times.

Mathews was handicapped playing in County Stadium, a tough home run park for lefthanded hitters. His career home park homer percentage was 46, lowest of anyone in the 500 Club.

No. 500: Mathews has the distinction of being the only player to hit his 500th off a Hall of Famer: Juan Marichal of the Giants (July 14, 1967). Mathews was 35 and in his 16th season.

Etcetera: Mathews finished his career with Detroit in 1968. He hit his last two homers in the same game, then suffered a slipped disc climbing out of bed the next morning and never really came back.

Mathews was managing the Atlanta Braves in 1974 when his former teammate, Hank Aaron, broke Ruth's career record. Mathews offered the clubhouse toast: "To the best home-run hitter and best ballplayer who ever lived."

Other Views: Dixie Walker, minor league manager: "Mathews has as much power as either Babe Ruth or Ted Williams and they were in a class by themselves. Before he's through, this kid could write a new record book."

Paul Waner, Hall of Famer: "There' nothing I can teach Eddie Mathews. He's a natural hitter."

Ernie Banks

Position: Shortstop, First Baseman
Height, Weight: 6-1, 180
Batted: Right
Born: Jan. 31, 1931 in Dallas.

Currently: Sales representative for a moving van company in Los Angeles.

Background: Banks was one of 11 children. His father was a janitor with a wholesale grocery company and he encouraged Ernie to pursue a career in athletics.

In high school, Banks was an end in football, a guard in basketball (averaging 18 points per game), and a high jumper in track. He showed enough promise in baseball to sign with the Kansas City Monarchs of the Negro American League at age 19.

Recalling his days with the Monarchs, Banks said: "Ten, 15, maybe 20 thousand miles a year and our biggest night was in Hastings, Neb. We got $15 apiece." After two years in the Army, Banks became the first black player to sign with the Chicago Cubs.

Career Highlights: Banks became the first National Leaguer to win back-to-back MVP Awards (1958-59), playing both years for losing Cubs teams. He won the league home run title in 1958 (47) and 1960 (41).

Banks was an underrated defensive shortstop. He won the Gold Glove at the position in 1960 when he led the league in putouts, assists, doubleplays and fielding percentage. He beat out a pure glove man, Cincinnati's Roy McMillan.

Banks switched to first base in 1962 when a knee injury cut down on his range. He remained a dangerous hitter, especially in Wrigley Field, where he hit 290 of his career home runs.

No. 500: Banks hit his 500th off Atlanta's Pat Jarvis on May 12, 1970. "This is a tremendous relief to me and my family," Banks said. He was 39 and in his 18th season.

Etcetera: Known as "Mr. Cub," Banks was the most popular player in the history of the franchise. He was a buoyant spirit whose standard pregame greeting was, "It's a beautiful day. Let's play two."

Banks's hitting improved dramatically in his third major league season when he switched from a 35-ounce bat to 31-ounce. He found he could follow the pitch until the last instant, then pick it off with a quick stroke.

Other Views: Bill James: "In Banks, you've got a Gold

Hank Aaron 755

Babe Ruth 714

Willie Mays   660

Frank Robinson   586

Harmon Killebrew   573

Reggie Jackson 549

Mickey Mantle 536

Jimmie Foxx 534

Mike Schmidt 525

Ted Williams   521

Willie McCovey   521

Eddie Mathews 512

Ernie Banks 512

Mel Ott 511

Glove shortstop who hits over .300 with well over 40 home runs a year, driving in more runs than Jim Rice."

Manager Bob Scheffing: "I never heard Ernie make a boastful remark . . . After he hits a homer, he comes back to the bench looking as if he did something wrong."

Mel Ott

Position: Outfielder
Height, Weight: 5-9, 170
Batted: Left
Born: March 2, 1909 in Gretna, La.
Died: Nov. 21, 1958 in New Orleans
Background: Ott played high school football, basketball, and baseball, but his heart was in baseball, the game his father and uncle played successfully in the local semi-pro league.

At 16, Ott was a catcher and the first team he tried out for, the New Orleans Pelicans, cut him because he was so small. He caught on with a semi-pro team in Patterson, La., and the Giants invited him to a tryout in Sept., 1926.

Career Highlights: Ott signed with the Giants for $400 and blossomed into the National League's most feared power hitter. He won six league home run crowns aided by his cozy Polo Grounds home.

A pull hitter, Ott took dead aim on the right-field fence, just 257 feet away at the foul line. He hit 323 of his home runs at the Polo Grounds, 188 away. In some people's minds that taints his membership in the 500 Club.

This is not to say Ott was without power. In his first at-bat in the 1933 World Series, Ott hit a 420-foot homer off Washington's Walter Stewart, a lefthander. Ott hit .389 in that series as the Giants won, 4 games to 1.

No. 500: Ott hit his 500th off Boston's John Hutchings on Aug. 1, 1945. He was 36 and in his 20th season.

Etcetera: In his later years, Ott had trouble with his short, thick legs. For a while, he nursed them with vitamin injections. Finally, he resorted to olive-oil rubdowns before every game.

Ott could not run at all (he never had more than 10 stolen

bases in a season) but he was a good defensive player. He had a strong arm and a knack for playing the short rightfield wall like a billiards champ.

Ott was a colorful player who was nicknamed Master Melvin because of his innocent demeanor. He had an odd batting stance; as the pitcher was ready to deliver Ott lifted his front leg.

Other Views: Pie Traynor, Hall of Famer: "The best players are those who win the most games and I can't name another player who has exerted as strong an influence upon so many games [as Ott]."

Hank Aaron

Year	Team	G	AB	R	H	2B	3B	HR	RBI	BB	SO	Avg.
1954	Milwaukee	122	468	58	131	27	6	13	69	28	39	.280
1955	Milwaukee	153	602	105	189	37	9	27	106	49	61	.314
1956	Milwaukee	153	609	106	200	34	14	26	92	37	54	.328
1957	Milwaukee	151	615	118	198	27	6	44	132	57	58	.322
1958	Milwaukee	153	601	109	196	34	4	30	95	59	49	.326
1959	Milwaukee	154	629	116	223	46	7	39	123	51	54	.355
1960	Milwaukee	153	590	102	172	20	11	40	126	60	63	.292
1961	Milwaukee	155	603	115	197	39	10	34	120	56	64	.327
1962	Milwaukee	156	592	127	191	28	6	45	128	66	73	.323
1963	Milwaukee	161	631	121	201	29	4	44	130	78	94	.319
1964	Milwaukee	145	570	103	187	30	2	24	95	62	46	.328
1965	Milwaukee	150	570	109	181	40	1	32	89	60	81	.318
1966	Atlanta	158	603	117	168	23	1	44	127	76	96	.279
1967	Atlanta	155	600	113	184	37	3	39	109	63	97	.307
1968	Atlanta	160	606	84	174	33	4	29	86	64	62	.287
1969	Atlanta	147	547	100	164	30	3	44	97	87	47	.300
1970	Atlanta	150	516	103	154	26	1	38	118	74	63	.298
1971	Atlanta	139	495	95	162	22	3	47	118	71	58	.327
1972	Atlanta	129	449	75	119	10	0	34	77	92	55	.265
1973	Atlanta	120	392	84	118	12	1	40	96	68	51	.301
1974	Atlanta	112	340	47	91	16	0	20	69	39	29	.268
1975	Milwaukee	137	465	45	109	16	2	12	60	70	51	.234
1976	Milwaukee	85	271	22	62	8	0	10	35	35	38	.229
Totals		3298	12364	2174	3771	624	98	755	2297	1402	1383	.305

Babe Ruth

Year	Team	G	AB	R	H	2B	3B	HR	RBI	BB	SO	Avg.
1914	Boston (A)	5	10	1	2	1	0	0	0	0	4	.200
1915	Boston (A)	42	92	16	29	10	1	4	21	9	23	.315
1916	Boston (A)	67	136	18	37	5	3	3	16	10	23	.272
1917	Boston (A)	52	123	14	40	6	3	2	12	12	18	.325
1918	Boston (A)	95	317	50	95	26	11	11	66	57	58	.300
1919	Boston (A)	130	432	103	139	34	12	29	114	101	58	.322
1920	New York (A)	142	458	158	172	36	9	54	137	148	80	.376
1921	New York (A)	152	540	177	204	44	16	59	171	144	81	.378
1922	New York (A)	110	406	94	128	24	8	35	99	84	80	.315
1923	New York (A)	152	522	151	205	45	13	41	131	170	93	.393
1924	New York (A)	153	529	143	200	39	7	46	121	142	81	.378
1925	New York (A)	98	359	61	104	12	2	25	66	59	68	.290
1926	New York (A)	152	495	139	184	30	5	47	145	144	76	.372
1927	New York (A)	151	540	158	192	29	8	60	164	138	89	.356
1928	New York (A)	154	536	163	173	29	8	54	142	135	87	.323
1929	New York (A)	135	499	121	172	26	6	46	154	72	60	.345
1930	New York (A)	145	518	150	186	28	9	49	153	136	61	.359
1931	New York (A)	145	534	149	199	31	3	46	163	128	51	.373
1932	New York (A)	133	457	120	156	13	5	41	137	130	62	.341
1933	New York (A)	137	459	97	138	21	3	34	103	114	90	.301
1934	New York (A)	125	365	78	105	17	4	22	84	103	63	.288
1935	New York (A)	28	72	13	13	0	0	6	12	20	24	.181
Totals		2503	8399	2174	2873	506	136	714	2211	2056	1330	.342

Willie Mays

Year	Team	G	AB	R	H	2B	3B	HR	RBI	BB	SO	Avg.
1951	New York (N)	121	464	59	127	22	5	20	68	56	60	.274
1952	New York (N)	34	127	17	30	2	4	4	23	16	17	.236
1954	New York (N)	151	565	119	195	33	13	41	110	66	57	.345
1955	New York (N)	152	580	123	185	18	13	51	127	79	60	.319
1956	New York (N)	152	578	101	171	27	8	36	84	68	65	.296
1957	New York (N)	152	585	112	195	26	20	35	97	76	62	.333
1958	San Francisco	152	600	121	208	33	11	29	96	78	56	.347
1959	San Francisco	151	575	125	180	43	5	34	104	65	58	.313
1960	San Francisco	153	595	107	190	29	12	29	103	61	70	.319
1961	San Francisco	154	572	129	176	32	3	40	123	81	77	.308
1962	San Francisco	162	621	130	189	36	5	49	141	78	85	.304
1963	San Francisco	157	596	115	187	32	7	38	103	66	83	.314
1964	San Francisco	157	578	121	171	21	9	47	111	82	72	.296
1965	San Francisco	157	558	118	177	21	3	52	112	76	71	.317
1966	San Francisco	152	552	99	159	29	4	37	103	70	81	.288
1967	San Francisco	141	486	83	128	22	2	22	70	51	92	.263
1968	San Francisco	148	498	84	144	20	5	23	79	67	81	.289
1969	San Francisco	117	403	64	114	17	3	13	58	49	71	.283
1970	San Francisco	139	478	94	139	15	2	28	83	79	90	.291
1971	San Francisco	136	417	82	113	24	5	18	61	112	123	.271
1972	S.F.-New York (N)	88	244	35	61	11	1	8	22	60	48	.250
1973	New York	66	209	24	44	10	0	6	25	27	47	.211
	Totals	2992	10881	2062	3283	523	140	660	1903	1463	1526	.302

Frank Robinson

Year	Team	G	AB	R	H	2B	3B	HR	RBI	BB	SO	Avg.
1956	Cincinnati	152	572	122	166	27	6	38	83	64	95	.290
1957	Cincinnati	150	611	97	197	29	5	29	75	44	92	.322
1958	Cincinnati	148	554	90	149	25	6	31	83	62	80	.269
1959	Cincinnati	146	540	106	168	31	4	36	125	69	93	.311
1960	Cincinnati	139	464	86	138	33	6	31	83	82	67	.297
1961	Cincinnati	153	545	117	176	32	7	37	124	71	64	.323
1962	Cincinnati	162	609	134	208	51	2	39	136	76	62	.342
1963	Cincinnati	140	482	79	125	19	3	21	91	81	69	.259
1964	Cincinnati	156	568	103	174	38	6	29	96	79	67	.306
1965	Cincinnati	156	582	109	172	33	5	33	113	70	100	.296
1966	Baltimore	155	576	122	182	34	2	49	122	87	90	.316
1967	Baltimore	129	479	83	149	23	7	30	94	71	84	.311
1968	Baltimore	130	421	69	113	27	1	15	52	73	84	.268
1969	Baltimore	148	539	111	166	19	5	32	100	88	62	.308
1970	Baltimore	132	471	88	144	24	1	25	78	69	70	.306
1971	Baltimore	133	455	82	128	16	2	28	99	72	62	.281
1972	Los Angeles	103	342	41	86	6	1	19	59	55	76	.251
1973	California	147	534	85	142	29	0	30	97	82	93	.266
1974	Calif.-Clev.	144	477	81	117	27	3	22	68	85	95	.245
1975	Cleveland	49	118	19	28	5	0	9	24	29	15	.237
1976	Cleveland	36	67	5	15	0	0	3	10	11	12	.224
	Totals	2808	10006	1829	2943	528	72	586	1812	1420	1532	.294

Harmon Killebrew

Year	Team	G	AB	R	H	2B	3B	HR	RBI	BB	SO	Avg.
1954	Washington	9	13	1	4	1	0	0	3	2	3	.308
1955	Washington	38	80	12	16	1	0	4	7	9	31	.200
1956	Washington	44	99	10	22	2	0	5	13	10	39	.222
1957	Washington	9	31	4	9	2	0	2	5	2	8	.290
1958	Washington	13	31	2	6	0	0	0	2	0	12	.194
1959	Washington	153	546	98	132	20	2	42	105	90	116	.242
1960	Washington	124	442	84	122	19	1	31	80	71	106	.276
1961	Minnesota	150	541	94	156	20	7	46	122	107	109	.288
1962	Minnesota	155	552	85	134	21	1	48	126	106	142	.243
1963	Minnesota	142	515	88	133	18	0	45	96	72	105	.258
1964	Minnesota	158	577	95	156	11	1	49	111	93	135	.270
1965	Minnesota	113	401	78	108	16	1	25	75	72	69	.269
1966	Minnesota	162	569	89	160	27	1	39	110	103	98	.281
1967	Minnesota	163	547	105	147	24	1	44	113	131	111	.269
1968	Minnesota	100	295	40	62	7	2	17	40	70	70	.210
1969	Minnesota	162	555	106	153	20	2	49	140	145	84	.276
1970	Minnesota	157	527	96	143	20	1	41	113	128	84	.271
1971	Minnesota	147	500	61	127	19	1	28	119	114	96	.254
1972	Minnesota	139	433	53	100	13	2	26	74	94	91	.231
1973	Minnesota	69	248	29	60	9	1	5	32	41	59	.242
1974	Minnesota	122	333	28	74	7	0	13	54	45	61	.222
1975	Kansas City	106	312	25	62	13	0	14	44	54	70	.199
	Totals	2435	8147	1283	2086	290	24	573	1584	1559	1699	.256

Reggie Jackson

Year	Team	G	AB	R	H	2B	3B	HR	RBI	BB	SO	Avg.
1967	Kansas City	35	118	13	21	4	4	1	6	10	46	.178
1968	Oakland	154	553	82	138	13	0	29	74	50	171	.250
1969	Oakland	152	549	123	151	36	3	47	118	114	142	.275
1970	Oakland	149	426	57	101	21	2	23	66	75	135	.237
1971	Oakland	150	567	87	157	29	3	32	80	63	161	.277
1972	Oakland	135	499	72	132	25	2	25	75	59	125	.265
1973	Oakland	151	539	99	158	28	2	32	117	76	111	.293
1974	Oakland	148	506	90	146	25	1	29	93	86	105	.289
1975	Oakland	157	593	91	150	39	3	36	104	67	133	.253
1976	Baltimore	134	498	84	138	27	2	27	91	54	108	.277
1977	New York (A)	146	525	93	150	39	2	32	110	75	129	.286
1978	New York (A)	139	511	82	140	13	5	27	97	58	133	.274
1979	New York (A)	131	465	78	138	24	2	29	89	65	107	.297
1980	New York (A)	143	514	94	154	22	4	41	111	83	122	.300
1981	New York (A)	94	334	33	79	17	1	15	54	46	82	.237
1982	California	153	530	92	146	17	1	39	101	85	156	.275
1983	California	116	397	43	77	14	1	14	49	52	140	.194
1984	California	143	525	67	117	17	2	25	81	55	141	.223
1985	California	143	460	64	116	27	0	27	85	78	138	.252
1986	California	132	419	65	101	12	2	18	58	92	115	.241
1987	Oakland	115	336	42	74	14	1	15	43	33	97	.220
	Totals	2820	9864	1551	2584	463	49	563	1702	1376	2597	.262

Mickey Mantle

Year	Team	G	AB	R	H	2B	3B	HR	RBI	BB	SO	Avg.
1951	New York (A)	96	341	61	91	11	5	13	65	43	74	.267
1952	New York (A)	142	549	94	171	37	7	23	87	75	111	.311
1953	New York (A)	127	461	105	136	24	3	21	92	79	90	.295
1954	New York (A)	146	543	129	163	17	12	27	102	102	107	.300
1955	New York (A)	147	517	121	158	25	11	37	99	113	97	.306
1956	New York (A)	150	533	132	188	22	5	52	130	112	99	.353
1957	New York (A)	144	474	121	173	28	6	34	94	146	75	.365
1958	New York (A)	150	519	127	158	21	1	42	97	129	120	.304
1959	New York (A)	144	541	104	154	23	4	31	75	94	126	.285
1960	New York (A)	153	527	119	145	17	6	40	94	111	125	.275
1961	New York (A)	153	514	132	163	16	6	54	128	126	112	.317
1962	New York (A)	123	377	96	121	15	1	30	89	122	78	.321
1963	New York (A)	65	172	40	54	8	0	15	35	40	32	.314
1964	New York (A)	143	465	92	141	25	2	35	111	99	102	.303
1965	New York (A)	122	361	44	92	12	1	19	46	73	76	.255
1966	New York (A)	108	333	40	96	12	1	23	56	57	76	.288
1967	New York (A)	144	440	63	108	17	0	22	55	107	113	.245
1968	New York (A)	144	435	57	103	14	1	18	54	106	97	.237
Totals		2401	8102	1677	2415	344	72	536	1509	1734	1710	.298

Jimmie Foxx

Year	Team	G	AB	R	H	2B	3B	HR	RBI	BB	SO	Avg.
1925	Philadelphia (A)	10	9	2	6	1	0	0	0	0	1	.667
1926	Philadelphia (A)	26	32	8	10	2	1	0	5	1	6	.313
1927	Philadelphia (A)	61	130	23	42	6	5	3	20	14	11	.323
1928	Philadelphia (A)	118	400	85	131	29	10	13	79	60	43	.328
1929	Philadelphia (A)	149	517	123	183	23	9	33	117	103	70	.354
1930	Philadelphia (A)	153	562	127	188	33	13	37	156	93	66	.335
1931	Philadelphia (A)	139	515	93	150	32	10	30	120	73	84	.291
1932	Philadelphia (A)	154	585	151	213	33	9	58	169	116	96	.364
1933	Philadelphia (A)	149	573	125	204	37	9	48	163	96	93	.356
1934	Philadelphia (A)	150	539	120	180	28	6	44	130	111	75	.334
1935	Philadelphia (A)	147	535	118	185	33	7	36	115	114	99	.346
1936	Boston (A)	155	585	130	198	32	8	41	143	105	119	.338
1937	Boston (A)	150	569	111	162	24	6	36	127	99	96	.285
1938	Boston (A)	149	565	139	197	33	9	50	175	119	76	.349
1939	Boston (A)	124	467	130	168	31	10	35	105	89	72	.360
1940	Boston (A)	144	515	106	153	30	4	36	119	101	87	.297
1941	Boston (A)	135	487	87	146	27	8	19	105	93	103	.300
1942	Bost. (A)-Chi. (N)	100	305	43	69	12	0	8	33	40	70	.226
1944	Chicago (N)	15	20	0	1	0	0	0	2	2	5	.050
1945	Philadelphia (N)	89	224	30	60	11	1	7	38	23	39	.268
Totals		2317	8134	1751	2646	458	125	534	1921	1452	1311	.325

Ted Williams

Year	Team	G	AB	R	H	2B	3B	HR	RBI	BB	SO	Avg.
1939	Boston (A)	149	565	131	185	44	11	31	145	107	64	.327
1940	Boston (A)	144	561	134	193	43	14	23	113	96	54	.344
1941	Boston (A)	143	456	135	185	33	3	37	120	145	27	.406
1942	Boston (A)	150	522	141	186	34	5	36	137	145	51	.356
1946	Boston (A)	150	514	142	176	37	8	38	123	156	44	.342
1947	Boston (A)	156	528	125	181	40	9	32	114	162	47	.343
1948	Boston (A)	137	509	124	188	44	3	25	127	126	41	.369
1949	Boston (A)	155	566	150	194	39	3	43	159	162	48	.343
1950	Boston (A)	89	334	82	106	24	1	28	97	82	21	.317
1951	Boston (A)	148	531	109	169	28	4	30	126	144	45	.318
1952	Boston (A)	6	10	2	4	0	1	1	3	2	2	.400
1953	Boston (A)	37	91	17	37	6	0	13	34	19	10	.407
1954	Boston (A)	117	386	93	133	23	1	29	89	136	32	.345
1955	Boston (A)	98	320	77	114	21	3	28	83	91	24	.356
1956	Boston (A)	136	400	71	138	28	2	24	82	102	39	.345
1957	Boston (A)	132	420	96	163	28	1	38	87	119	43	.388
1958	Boston (A)	129	411	81	135	23	2	26	85	98	49	.328
1959	Boston (A)	103	272	32	69	15	0	10	43	52	27	.254
1960	Boston (A)	113	310	56	98	15	0	29	72	75	41	.316
Totals		2292	7706	1798	2654	525	71	521	1839	2019	709	.344

Willie McCovey

Year	Team	G	AB	R	H	2B	3B	HR	RBI	BB	SO	Avg.
1959	San Francisco	52	192	32	68	9	5	13	38	22	35	.354
1960	San Francisco	101	260	37	62	15	3	13	51	45	53	.238
1961	San Francisco	106	328	59	89	12	3	18	50	37	60	.271
1962	San Francisco	91	229	41	67	6	1	20	54	29	35	.293
1963	San Francisco	152	564	103	158	19	5	44	102	50	119	.280
1964	San Francisco	130	364	55	80	14	1	18	54	61	73	.220
1965	San Francisco	160	540	93	149	17	4	39	92	88	118	.276
1966	San Francisco	150	502	85	148	26	6	36	96	76	100	.295
1967	San Francisco	135	456	73	126	17	4	31	91	71	110	.276
1968	San Francisco	148	523	81	153	16	4	36	105	72	71	.293
1969	San Francisco	149	491	101	157	26	2	45	126	121	66	.320
1970	San Francisco	152	495	98	143	39	2	39	126	137	75	.289
1971	San Francisco	105	329	45	91	13	0	18	70	64	57	.277
1972	San Francisco	81	263	30	56	8	0	14	35	38	45	.213
1973	San Francisco	130	383	52	102	14	3	29	75	105	78	.266
1974	San Diego	128	344	53	87	19	1	22	63	96	76	.253
1975	San Diego	122	413	43	104	17	0	23	68	57	80	.252
1976	S.D.-Oakland	82	226	20	46	9	0	7	36	24	43	.204
1977	San Francisco	141	478	54	134	21	0	28	86	67	106	.280
1978	San Francisco	108	351	32	80	19	2	12	64	36	57	.228
1979	San Francisco	117	353	34	88	9	0	15	57	36	70	.249
1980	San Francisco	48	113	8	23	8	0	1	16	13	23	.204
Totals		2588	8197	1229	2211	353	46	521	1555	1345	1550	.270

Eddie Mathews

Year	Team	G	AB	R	H	2B	3B	HR	RBI	BB	SO	Avg.
1952	Boston (N)	145	528	80	128	23	5	25	58	59	115	.242
1953	Milwaukee	154	579	110	175	31	8	47	135	99	83	.302
1954	Milwaukee	138	476	96	138	21	4	40	103	113	61	.290
1955	Milwaukee	141	499	108	144	23	5	41	101	109	98	.289
1956	Milwaukee	151	552	103	150	21	2	37	95	91	86	.272
1957	Milwaukee	148	572	109	167	28	9	32	94	90	79	.292
1958	Milwaukee	149	546	97	137	18	1	31	77	85	85	.251
1959	Milwaukee	148	594	118	182	16	8	46	114	80	71	.306
1960	Milwaukee	153	548	108	152	19	7	39	124	111	113	.277
1961	Milwaukee	152	572	103	175	23	6	32	91	93	95	.306
1962	Milwaukee	152	536	106	142	25	6	29	90	101	90	.265
1963	Milwaukee	158	547	82	144	27	4	23	84	124	119	.263
1964	Milwaukee	141	502	83	117	19	1	23	74	85	100	.233
1965	Milwaukee	156	546	77	137	23	0	32	95	73	110	.251
1966	Atlanta	134	452	72	113	21	4	16	53	63	82	.250
1967	Houston-Detroit	137	436	53	103	16	2	16	57	63	88	.236
1968	Detroit	31	52	4	11	0	0	3	8	5	12	.212
	Totals	2388	8537	1509	2315	354	72	512	1453	1444	1487	.271

Ernie Banks

Year	Team	G	AB	R	H	2B	3B	HR	RBI	BB	SO	Avg.
1953	Chicago (N)	10	35	3	11	1	1	2	6	4	5	.314
1954	Chicago (N)	154	593	70	163	19	7	19	79	40	50	.275
1955	Chicago (N)	154	596	98	176	29	9	44	117	45	72	.295
1956	Chicago (N)	139	538	82	160	25	8	28	85	52	62	.297
1957	Chicago (N)	156	594	113	169	34	6	43	102	70	85	.285
1958	Chicago (N)	154	617	119	193	23	11	47	129	52	87	.313
1959	Chicago (N)	155	589	97	179	25	6	45	143	64	72	.304
1960	Chicago (N)	156	597	94	162	32	7	41	117	71	69	.271
1961	Chicago (N)	138	511	75	142	22	4	29	80	54	75	.278
1962	Chicago (N)	154	610	87	164	20	6	37	104	30	71	.269
1963	Chicago (N)	130	432	41	98	20	1	18	64	39	73	.227
1964	Chicago (N)	157	591	67	156	29	6	23	95	36	84	.264
1965	Chicago (N)	163	612	79	162	25	3	28	106	55	64	.265
1966	Chicago (N)	141	511	52	139	23	7	15	75	29	59	.272
1967	Chicago (N)	151	573	68	158	26	4	23	95	27	93	.276
1968	Chicago (N)	150	552	71	136	27	0	32	83	27	67	.246
1969	Chicago (N)	155	565	60	143	19	2	23	106	42	101	.253
1970	Chicago (N)	72	222	25	56	6	2	12	44	20	33	.252
1971	Chicago (N)	39	83	4	16	2	0	3	6	6	14	1.93
	Totals	2528	9421	1305	2583	407	90	512	1636	763	1236	2.74

Mel Ott

Year	Team	G	AB	R	H	2B	3B	HR	RBI	BB	SO	Avg.
1926	New York (N)	35	60	7	23	2	0	0	4	1	9	.383
1927	New York (N)	82	163	23	46	7	3	1	19	13	9	.282
1928	New York (N)	124	435	69	140	26	4	18	77	52	36	.322
1929	New York (N)	150	545	138	179	37	2	42	151	113	38	.328
1930	New York (N)	148	521	122	182	34	5	25	119	103	35	.349
1931	New York (N)	138	497	104	145	23	8	29	115	80	44	.292
1932	New York (N)	154	566	119	180	30	8	38	123	100	39	.318
1933	New York (N)	152	580	98	164	36	1	23	103	75	48	.283
1934	New York (N)	153	582	119	190	29	10	35	135	85	43	.326
1935	New York (N)	152	593	113	191	33	6	31	114	82	58	.322
1936	New York (N)	150	534	120	175	28	6	33	135	102	41	.328
1937	New York (N)	151	545	99	160	28	2	31	95	102	69	.294
1938	New York (N)	152	527	116	164	23	6	36	116	118	47	.311
1939	New York (N)	125	396	85	122	23	2	27	80	100	50	.308
1940	New York (N)	151	536	89	155	27	3	19	79	100	50	.289
1941	New York (N)	148	525	89	150	29	0	27	90	100	68	.286
1942	New York (N)	152	549	118	162	21	0	30	93	109	61	.295
1943	New York (N)	125	380	65	89	12	2	18	47	95	48	.234
1944	New York (N)	120	399	91	115	16	4	26	82	90	47	.288
1945	New York (N)	135	451	73	139	23	0	21	79	71	41	.308
1946	New York (N)	31	2	68	5	1	0	1	4	8	15	.074
1947	New York (N)	4	4	0	0	0	0	0	0	0	0	.000
	Totals	2732	9456	1859	2876	488	72	511	1860	1708	896	.304

When They Got To 500 ...

The following are the total number of seasons, games and at-bats for each player at the time of his 500th career home run:

SEASONS		GAMES		AT-BATS	
Willie Mays	14	Babe Ruth	1740	Babe Ruth	5800
Henry Aaron	15	Harmon Killebrew	1955	Harmon Killebrew	6671
Mike Schmidt	16	Jimmie Foxx	1971	Jimmie Foxx	7075
Babe Ruth	16	Willie Mays	1987	Mickey Mantle	7300
Jimmie Foxx	16	Mike Schmidt	2118	Mike Schmidt	7331
Frank Robinson	16	Mickey Mantle	2136	Billy Williams	7454
Eddie Mathews	16	Henry Aaron	2204	Willie Mays	7533
Mickey Mantle	17	Billy Williams	2210	Willie McCovey	7582
Reggie Jackson	17	Eddie Mathews	2291	Eddie Mathews	8280
Harmon Killebrew	18	Frank Robinson	2315	Frank Robinson	8427
Ernie Banks	18	Willie McCovey	2377	Reggie Jackson	8599
Billy Williams	19	Reggie Jackson	2417	Henry Aaron	8612
Mel Ott	20	Ernie Banks	2442	Ernie Banks	9204
Willie McCovey	20	Mel Ott	2660	Mel Ott	9273

A SOFT SPOT FOR MASTER MELVIN

BY STAN HOCHMAN

Mel Ott. Master Melvin, the sports writers called him, because he was boyish, innocent, country.

Square jaw. Little guy, maybe 5-9, possibly 170, although it was hard to tell because the uniforms were woolly and baggy in those days.

Did I idolize him because he was a little guy or because I was a little guy?

What was he, 16, when he showed up for spring training with the Giants? Carried his clothing in a cardboard suitcase? I'm not going to look it up, to check it for accuracy. This is the way I remember it, this is the way I want to remember it.

He had a unique way of hitting. Lifted that front foot as the pitcher released the ball. Plopped it down, transferred his weight, lashed at the ball, sent it soaring.

Did I idolize him because he dared to be different? Because he was still a teenager when he got to the big leagues, which meant all dreams were possible? Because he showed up with a cardboard suitcase, which meant poor and unworldly, which is what I was?

I became a Mel Ott fan. Not a Giants' fan. I didn't know you had to root for an entire team, not just one ballplayer. We did not talk baseball at our dinner table.

Irving Scharf, he was a Giants' fan. He could listen to the ballgame on the radio and in the eighth inning, before the announcer said it, he could tell you that Dick Bartell was 2-for-4, with two runs batted in. He knew who was going to pinch-hit for the pitcher and who would stalk in from the bullpen the next inning.

Me, I only knew Ott's statistics and could mimick the way he hit. Until the ball arrived. I saved his baseball bubblegum card even when I gambled away the others, playing blackjack on the sticky tar roof of our apartment building in Brooklyn.

I think he hit 42 homers one year and he should have tied Chuck Klein for the league title. The Giants finished the season with a doubleheader at Baker Bowl and Klein hit one off King Carl Hubbell in the first game to give him 43 and the Phillies walked Ott three or four times in the nightcap, which is what we called the second game of a doubleheader.

I think the Giants had an eight- or nine-run lead in the ninth inning and the bases were jammed and Ott came up one more time. Fidgety Phil Collins was pitching and the Phillies made him walk Ott and force in a run rather than let Master Melvin swing and maybe hit another homer and tie Klein.

I remember how Ott used to paw at the ground in rightfield while the Giants' pitchers ran those dreary deep counts on hitters. By the end of a homestand, there was a drab, brown patch in rightfield.

I'd ride the Woodlawn-Jerome train, change at, what, 147th street? Anyway, walk down a steep flight of steps to the Polo Grounds. Sit on a backless bench in the bleachers, eat the lunch I'd brought in a brown paper bag between games of the doubleheader.

Watch the players trudge up the clubhouse steps in centerfield after games. Wait for them afterward, for a glimpse, for an autograph. Years later, I'd ride all the way back to Brooklyn on the subway with Sid Gordon because he lived around the corner, on St. John's Place.

Ott hit a lot of homers in the Polo Grounds. It was 258 feet down the lines. The sports writers called 260-foot homers "Chinese" homers and I never understood why.

I was sad when the Giants made Ott the manager. I thought he was too young, too gentle, and that the players would take advantage of him. They did.

And then the Giants replaced him with Leo Durocher in the middle of the 1948 season and I never rooted for the Giants again. I rooted for Brooklyn, until the Dodgers moved to California.

By then I was a sports writer and I couldn't root for whole teams, just for some individual good guys.

Ott was killed in a head-on collision on a foggy highway years later. The only time he was mentioned after that was when Sadaharu Oh hit all those homers in Japan, with that same one-legged angry flamingo stance.

And now? Now that Mike Schmidt has moved past Ott, the man who was closest to him on the all-time home run list with 511? The memories come flooding back, of growing up in Brooklyn, of riding the musty subway, of brown paper bag lunches, bleachers, and the raw brown patch in rightfield where Ott pawed the grass.

And then I scanned the list of the other guys with more homers than Ott, and I realized how lucky I have been, to have shared moments of triumph and sadness with so many of them.

I saw Henry Aaron (755) play the very first integrated baseball game in Augusta, Ga.

He was playing second base for Jacksonville and he hit a homer his first time up, a line drive that scorched over the centerfield fence.

And then his team took the field and the yahoos in the rightfield bleachers started throwing rocks at the rightfielder, a black man named Warner.

The umpires conferred with both managers and, finally, a compromise was worked out. Warner was moved to leftfield, to play in the safe shadow of the "colored" bleachers.

I wrote a story for the Augusta paper referring to the rightfield patrons as lunatic fringe. I lasted one more week. Aaron went on to be the league's MVP.

I was there, through most of a rainy September in 1973, as he approached Ruth's 714. Groping for a fresh question, I asked him if all the pressure was affecting his sex life. He laughed.

We were going to go fishing, but somehow it never happened.

We have remained friends. We have spoken only once of that ugly night in Augusta.

Babe Ruth (714) was in a Dodgers uniform when I saw my first major league ballgame at Ebbets Field.

Burleigh Grimes was the manager and when he came out to argue a call he put a bandana over the bottom half of his face, like Jesse James.

Ruth coached first, waddling on those spindly legs, relaying signals like a man playing charades with 8-year-olds.

A couple of years later, I had my first summer job, billing clerk at a Yorktown harberdashery. Going through the accounts, there it was, George Herman Ruth, three shirts, two ties. My palms were sweaty.

He never appeared in the store that summer. The next time I saw him, it was in newsreels of his raspy farewell speech at Yankee Stadium, wearing that camel's hair cap, that big overcoat.

I was there when Willie Mays (660) whirled and threw out Billy Cox at home plate in Ebbets Field, the finest throw I've ever seen.

By the time I started covering the Phillies in '59 Mays was wary, aloof. He loosened up later on, then retreated into grumpiness as his skills deteriorated.

He seemed happy last year, traveling with the Giants, chirping in the clubhouse.

I was there when Frank Robinson (586) stepped aside to let Chico Ruiz steal home against the Phillies in 1964, starting that 10-game skid.

Robinson had that brazen way of hitting, with his head over the plate, scowling out at the pitcher over his bicep.

I remember that Gene Mauch had forbidden his pitchers from knocking down Robinson because of all the damage Robinson would do when he got back up.

I remember a three-hit game-winning night after the Phillies had conned Robinson into a rare baserunning mistake with a "phantom" doubleplay pantomime the night before.

And I remember a tawdry brawl matching Robinson and Robin Roberts.

I hardly knew Harmon Killebrew (573) because he played in obscurity, which is a suburb of Minneapolis.

We all know Reggie Jackson (563). How could we not

know him? He had been woeful in playoff games and wonderful in the World Series, thus becoming Mr. October.

He remembers writers' names and knows morning paper guys from afternoon paper guys and columnists from beat writers and he can charm you with his eloquence and sicken you with his cruelty.

I was there when he hit those three homers in one World Series game and I was glad he played in Oakland for one last year.

At the World Series, the writers always formed a distant semi-circle in front of Mickey Mantle (536). Not out of fear, but simply to make room for him to unwind all those yards of tape from his battered knees.

His family history is shadowed by tragedy and there is truth to his jest if he knew he was going to live this long, he would have taken better care of himself.

It is fascinating to watch him move among strangers now, bemused at his popularity, the kid from Oklahoma who survived the culture shock of New York.

I never knew Jimmie Foxx (534).

I knew only what I'd read about Ted Williams (521) and I didn't like him shooting ballpark pigeons with a rifle or spitting toward the press box. I did read, again and again, John McPhee's story on Williams's final game.

McPhee writes the way Williams hit.

I was there, in Seals Stadium, downwind from the brewery, when Willie McCovey (521) broke in with a four-hit day against Robin Roberts.

"Hit every fence, touched every base," said Gary Schumacher, the Giants' publicist. They don't make publicists like that anymore. They don't make sluggers like McCovey anymore.

He smoked a line drive that Bobby Richardson caught and the Yankees won the World Series. McCovey became known for that linedrive out instead of the 521 homers, the stoic way he played the game in sickness and in health.

He was a guest at my wedding. We keep in touch.

Ernie Banks (512) and Eddie Mathews (512) are tied for 11th place on the list, as different as daybreak and dusk.

Banks was a chatterbox. He remembered your name, was

always babbling about "the friendly confines of Wrigley Field." Always yipping "Let's play two" when only one was scheduled.

Some of his teammates called him "FOS" behind his back, an abbreviation for Full of Soup. But he was always cheerful, always courteous, and he could hit.

Mathews was somber, closed-mouthed, a brawler, overshadowed in that Braves' lineup by Aaron, Joe Adcock, Del Crandall.

He managed the Braves later on. Carried whiskey bottles and glasses in one of those sturdy travel cases you associate with tailgate parties.

Got caught in the crossfire of controversy the year Aaron hit 715, because the commissioner wanted Aaron to play in earlier games, on the road, and the Braves owner wanted Henry to sit them out.

I was there when he hit 715. Aaron signed my scoresheet. It's the only baseball autograph I've asked for in the last 15 years.

And now I've seen Michael Jack Schmidt overcome the trauma of a .196 rookie season to win the Most Valuable Player award three times, to win 10 Gold Gloves, to hit 500 home runs.

I hope he plays three more years, hits 100 more homers.

The Polo Grounds is rubble, the fields are made of plastic, but some things have not changed. I still root for the good guys.

SLUGGERS SALUTE SCHMIDT

BY RAY DIDINGER

Eddie Mathews was managing the Atlanta Braves when Mike Schmidt broke in with the Phillies in 1972. Schmidt didn't have the mustache then, or the stats, but he had everything else.

"He was a good-looking prospect," Mathews said. "Big and strong, but real fluid. He had a lot of pop. The ball came off his bat like a rocket.

"I can't say I looked at him and said, 'Here's a future Hall of Famer.' Too many things can happen. Injuries, off-the-field stuff. But I thought he was a kid with a helluva lot of tools and a chance to be something special."

Schmidt is something special now, the 14th player in major league history to hit 500 home runs. It is a select fraternity that includes just one other career third baseman, namely Eddie Mathews (512).

Mathews has held most National League records at the position since his retirement in 1968. By 1986, Schmidt already had wiped out one Mathews record (47 homers in a season by a third baseman) and he eclipsed several others last season.

Mathews, 55, takes it in stride. The Hall of Famer now works as a minor league instructor with the Braves. His job is to educate the top prospects in the art of hitting a baseball. If they go on to break his seven club records, well, that is the way it goes.

"If Schmidt passes me, more power to him," Mathews said before Schmidt's 500th homer. "I'm not going to cry about it.

That's baseball. He won't be taking anything away from me, anymore than Hank [Aaron] took anything away from Babe Ruth when he set the home run record.

"I don't think players put that much stock in numbers. Maybe some do, I never did. I could see a few years ago that Schmidt was going to blow by me if he stayed healthy. I didn't mind because I think Schmidt is a helluva player.

"If someone had to beat me out, I'm glad it was a guy like that . . . an all-around player who could do the job defensively as well as swing the bat. That's the kind of player I tried to be, a guy who did the job day-in and day-out."

There are many similarities between Mathews and Schmidt.
- Size: Mathews is 6-1 and played at 195 pounds; Schmidt is 6-2 and 200. Both were football stars in high school: Mathews in Santa Barbara, Calif., and Schmidt in Dayton, Ohio.
- Speed: Mathews was one of the National League's 10 fastest players in the '50s. He was clocked from home to first in 3.5 seconds. Schmidt needs just 18 stolen bases to pass Garry Maddox for fifth place on the Phillies' all-time list.
- Whiffs: Mathews led the National League with 115 strikeouts as a rookie in 1952. Schmidt led the league in strikeouts three straight years (1974-76). He also led the league in homers the same three seasons.

Also, their batting averages are almost identical. Mathews hit .271 in 17 seasons with the Braves, Houston and Detroit. Schmidt has a .270 mark for 15 seasons.

Schmidt was the better fielder, but Mathews developed into a better-than-average gloveman.

One interesting contrast is their home run pace.

Mathews had the most auspicious start of any 500 Clubber: 153 homers in his first four seasons. Several notables, including Hall of Famer Ralph Kiner, predicted Mathews would break Ruth's record of 714. But Mathews slowed in his 30s, averaging 21 homers his last eight seasons.

Schmidt has grown stronger with age. He closed the gap between homers No. 300 and 500 faster than any hitter with the exception of Aaron and Ruth. Mathews can appreciate that more than anyone.

"You take a beating at third base," Mathews said. "You get hot shots off your hands, you get spiked making tags.

Physically, it wears you down. That's why you don't see many third basemen on that [home run] list.

"For Schmidt to play this long and still be leading the league in home runs . . . that's a helluva feat. I've got to tip my hat to him."

■

The 500 Clubbers, infielders and outfielders alike, have received Schmidt warmly. That is quite a tribute. As baseball peer groups go, this one is, well, peerless.

Even the immortals who never have met Schmidt have admired him from afar. Harmon Killebrew, the ex-Twin, is awed by Schmidt's 10 Gold Gloves. Killer played third base for half of his career but never dazzled anyone with his defense.

"Schmidt plays the position better than some guys who were strictly glove men," Killebrew said, "and he leads the league in home runs besides. Guys like Schmidt and [the Yankees' Don] Mattingly, you just love to watch."

Former Yankee great Mickey Mantle watches Schmidt on TV and marvels at the way the Phils' slugger seems to get better every year.

"He used to chase more bad pitches than he does now," Mantle said. "He looks more relaxed at the plate. I think he could be productive for a few more years. I could see him hitting 600 homers one of these days."

Aaron, the all-time home run champ, came to Veterans Stadium last September for a ceremony honoring Schmidt. The two talked at length about the adjustments a power hitter must make in his later years.

Aaron had three 40-plus home run seasons after the age of 35. He broke Ruth's career record when he was 40. It's all a matter of letting the mind pick up where the body leaves off.

"I didn't realize Schmidt was such a student of hitting," Aaron said. "He told me what he had done, moving up on the plate so he could pull the ball more. I dropped my hands so I could get them around quicker.

"I wished [Schmidt] luck going for 500. He seemed to have it in proper perspective. He said he wanted to enjoy the chase and that's the right attitude. You can't let all the hoopla distract you.

"I've always liked Schmidt," Aaron said. "I thought he was a real big leaguer. By that I mean he played the game very well in all phases and he carried himself with a lot of class. I didn't think he got the credit he deserved until the Phillies won the Series (1980)."

Willie McCovey, the former Giant star, agreed.

"I sympathized with the abuse Schmidt got in Philly all those years," McCovey said. "I went through the same thing in San Francisco. I came in as a rookie and moved Orlando Cepeda, the favorite son, off first base.

"It was a big controversy: 'Who should stay? Who should go?' When Cepeda was traded [to St. Louis] the press wanted to know why it wasn't me. The fans took sides. It got so bad I looked forward to road trips just so I could get away.

"But you hang on long enough and things turn around. I left San Francisco for a while, then came back and I was like a landmark. Schmidt has gone through the same cycle: hero, anti-hero, back to hero. The fans love him now, right?"

Right, but why do so many sluggers have this love-hate relationship with the fans? Ted Williams had it in Boston, Frank Robinson in Cincinnati, Reggie Jackson in three cities.

"People expect you to hit a home run every time up," McCovey said "You don't do it, they feel like you're letting them down. But if you stick around a while, they appreciate what you're doing. Five hundred home runs is a whole lot of production."

■

Willie Mays doesn't remember, but Mick Schmidt does. It was the early '60s and Schmidt went to Crosley Field in Cincinnati with a Willie Mays poster and a pen, hoping for an autograph.

"I was waiting by the tunnel where the players came out," Schmidt said. "I saw Mays and said, 'Willie, Willie . . . sign this. Please.' He just kept on walking. It's funny how you never forget things like that."

Mays forgot, but that is understandable. Schmidt was just another freckled face in the crowd back then. Today, he is a three-time National League MVP and eight-time home run champion.

"I put Schmidt in the category of a true superstar," said

Mays, who won MVP Awards 11 years apart (1954, 1965) with the Giants. "He's one of the best all-around players I've seen and I've seen quite a few."

Mays played 22 seasons and retired after the 1973 World Series. He still was a legitimate power-hitter at 39: he had 28 homers and 83 RBI in 1970. Schmidt will not turn 38 until September. He is not through climbing the 500 ladder.

"Yeah, Schmidt can go on," Mays said. "He keeps himself in shape. He looks like a young man and he plays like a young man. He still has that same desire. That's important.

"This is a game of youth. A lot of players get old mentally before they get old physically. They lose their enthusiasm, it drags their whole game down. Schmidt looks good. He's loose, he's enjoying himself. It shows in his performance."

Mays, who produced a 3-yard career-high (1961, 1963) with the Giants. "He's one of the best at all-around players I've coached," said Quinn a test.

His should be a smash and earned after the 1971 WLAF Super Bowl, was a last-minute substitute at QB because Barnes suffered a rib in 1976. Benjamin took no more 'f' until yesterday. "It is our duty," he told the 200 fans on "every single pass we get," Mays said. "The Rogue line can't in any way be beaten like a vanguard... we have to play fair, just like his own teammates. Team. That's important. He is a great defender. A lot of players who do that are before they get old physically. They took their consent as a Grey Cup. "How came down to his full luck, we said..." Mike de Vera quit himself: "I always in his performance."

to score a touchdown is 109 yards, assuming a kick.

A CAREER OF GREAT CLOUT

BY BILL CONLIN

Swing and a long drive . . . There it is! . . . Number 500 . . . Career 500th home run for Mi-kull Jaaaaak Schmidttt.

Home run.
Four-ply swat.
Four-bagger.
Old-Goldie.
Downtown.
Moonshot.
Tape-measure job.
Holy Cow!
Hey-hey!

The Giants win the pennant! The Giants win the pennant! The Giants win the pennant! The Giants win the pennant! The Giants win the pennant!

It is the climactic stroke of sports: instant gratification for the offense; a jarring setback for the defense.

Home run. It is a significant term in the vocabulary of every American endeavor, from politics to young love—a term of endearment or of bereavement. German infiltrators dressed in U.S. infantry uniforms in the Battle of the Bulge were gunned down on the spot because they blew questions involving Babe Ruth.

The most a basketball can travel to score three points is about 90 feet. The longest distance a football player can run to score a touchdown is 109 yards, assuming a kick returner fields a ball on the endline of the end zone. The shortest is with the nose of the football almost touching the goal line.

But a baseball can be struck 420 feet and be a long out. Or it can travel less then 275 feet and take its place as one of the most dramatic home runs of all time.

Tape-measure job.

Wind-blown.

Moonshot.

Five-hundred-level rocket.

Into Greenberg's Gardens (also, Kiner's Korner). Or the Moondeck, Jury Box, Jonesville and other distant—and not-so-distant—reaches. The House That Ruth Built was not constructed of singles.

Home runs have made baseball a game of geography. In the modern game, we have the weathered survivors of a bygone age hanging on grimly against the synthetic in-roads of AstroTurf and closed, sterile, concentric, all-purpose circles.

The ballyards of Chicago, Detroit, Boston, Baltimore, Cleveland, and Milwaukee might lack parking. They might feature antiquated and inadequate facilities. But, by God, a baseball game between the Phillies and Chicago Cubs in Wrigley Field is a *baseball* game. When the New York Yankees and Boston Red Sox get together in Fenway Park, with the outfield angles of an architect gone mad, it is the closest the national pastime can offer to a religious experience. Fathers will tell sons from generation to generation about Bucky Dent and the home run that made all New England weep.

Michael Jack Schmidt hit another clutch home run. What else is new?

Many gifted athletes who are fortunate enough to survive the tests baseball imposes at every level, achieve an exalted status just by making it to the major leagues for one at-bat.

If they accomplish nothing else in life, people always will point and say, "He played in the big leagues."

A man with 50 at-bats had a cup of coffee. A man with 500 had brunch. A man who reaches 5,000 at-bats has had one hell of a career and reaches a special status even if his lifetime batting average is .230, even if his home run total is less than 100.

It takes a special blend of towering skill, incredible durability and an almost outrageous fortune to last the 12 years or so it takes most major leaguers to reach the 5,000 at-bat plateau.

Mike Schmidt has 500 home runs.

The achievement is so staggering that of all the thousands of players who have made it to the big leagues to appear in at least one game, Schmidt is just the 14th slugger to reach the 500 level—baseball's High Peaks Country.

If Schmidt plays two more seasons after this one—the Gold Glove third baseman says he will resign with the Phils but will not take a pay cut—and averages 30 home runs in each season, he will. Mantle (536), Reggie Jackson (563), Harmon Killebrew (573), and Frank Robinson (586). In 1987, with 35 home runs, Schmidt passed, in rapid succession, Mel Ott (511), Ernie Banks (512), Eddie Mathews (512), Willie McCovey (521), and Ted Williams (521).

It would appear that with good health, continued motivation to play and his increasing knowledge of the science of hitting that Schmidt has a fighting chance to pass all but the Big 3—Henry Aaron (755), Babe Ruth (714), and Willie Mays (660).

As he neared No. 500, Schmidt was gracious enough to block out some time during the tumult of the countdown to discuss some of the land-mark homers he has hit during the long march.

- A big one during his college career at Ohio University.
- No. 1 for the Phillies off Montreal righthander Balor Moore during a September callup from the minor leagues in 1972.
- Nos. 95, 96, 97, and 98 in Wrigley Field on April 17, 1976.
- No. 100 off Pirates lefthander John Candelaria on April 20, 1976.
- No. 200 off San Francisco Giants lefthander Vida Blue on May 13, 1979 in Candlestick Park.
- No. 283 off Montreal Expos righthander Stan Bahnsen in Olympic Stadium on Oct. 4, 1980, the 11th-inning blunderbolt that clinched the East Division title for the eventual World Series champions.
- No. 300 in Shea Stadium off a gangly New York Mets'

youngster named Mike Scott on Aug. 14, 1981. Yep, *that* Mike Scott.

- No. 400 in Dodger Stadium off flame-throwing righthander Bob Welch on May 15, 1984.
- No. 450 in Candlestick Park off former Phillies teammate Mike Krukow on Sept. 4, 1985.
- No. 495 in Three Rivers Stadium off rookie lefthander John Smiley last Sept. 22, the home run that began the official countdown to No. 500.

Ohio University vs. Bowling Green in a Mid-America Conference game late in the 1971 collegiate baseball season. Phillies farm director Paul Owens is zipped up in a windbreaker and seated next to area scout Tony Lucadello. They are there to watch a big, powerful shortstop. "He was a high first-round choice in every respect," Owens remembers, "but his knees had a lot of clubs scared off. He was back for his senior year and not a lot of college seniors are drafted No. 1. Lucadello said he was a No. 1 pick we might be able to steal as a No. 2. And that's how it turned out. On our reports we had Mike above big-league average in every category but arm and running speed. And he was nursing some minor injuries when we saw him and he wound up being above average in throwing and running, too."

The Bowling Green pitcher Schmidt homered off with Owens watching was a future major league reliever named Doug Bair. Ironically, Bair was in spring training with the Phillies this year as a non-roster pitcher.

"Tony Lucadello had gotten Paul Owens to travel to Athens, Ohio, for a weekend series against the Bowling Green team," Schmidt said, rewinding his mental videotape to 1971. "We got rained out, Paul had to stay over. I played shortstop in the doubleheader and hit one of our big home runs. So, I got to show Paul a home run, a defensive play in the hole, I took an extra base on a single. I did three real pivotal things they're looking for in a prospect. That's one I'll remember before becoming a professional because it helped the Phillies make a decision on me."

The Phillies started him at Reading in Class AA. When the

big club played its annual exhibition in the Eastern League city, Larry Bowa was ill and manager Frank Lucchesi borrowed Schmidt to play shortstop for the major leaguers.

"I hit a home run to win that game off of Mike Fremuth," Schmidt said. "That was a big one because it helped impress Paul Owens and Dallas Green that I belonged at Reading, when most of the new prospects were starting out in the rookie leagues and high A leagues. You're talking about a home run that saved me a year in my minor league career. I spent 1½ years in the minors as opposed to 2½, maybe 3 years. If that had happened, I'd be closing in on home run No. 460 or so."

They called him up in September of 1972 along with Bob Boone, Craig Robinson, and Mike Wallace. They were brought up to play; Schmidt was brought up to have knee surgery.

"They went with the club and I went to the hospital," Schmidt said. "They were going to operate on my left knee. The doctor was John Royal Moore, who used to be a famous orthopedic man in the city. He elected not to operate on it. He wanted to give me two or three weeks to see if it would heal up. The X-rays showed torn cartilage. He said he wanted me to go and see [trainer] Don Seger and do these exercises—this was before they had sophisticated rehabilitation techniques."

Four days later, Schmidt started at third base for Owens, who had become general manager in June and went down to the field after firing skipper Lucchesi.

"Balor Moore had 24 consecutive scoreless innings going for the Expos," Schmidt said. "We had a couple of men on base and I hit a three-run home run and I think we won the game, 3-2."

The next 18 homers were Schmidt's hardest. He dislocated his right shoulder diving for a ball at third near the end of spring training in 1973. When he returned to manager Danny Ozark's lineup, Schmidt was back on square one after staying behind in a Clearwater rehab program.

He remembers home run No. 2, however. "It beat Bob Gibson, 2-1, and I remember him walking off the field as the ball curled around the foul pole in left," Schmidt said. "Tim McCarver was the catcher."

The first grand slam?

"It was off a New York Mets pitcher named Phil Hennigan in Shea Stadium," Schmidt said, withdrawing that obscure journeyman from the bat rack of memory. "I hadn't hit one in about five years. But I had only hit with the bases loaded about five times in five years, too. And really, that's the only grand slam I remember. I have seven, but I only remember two of them."

So much for total recall. Schmidt's first grand slam was actually off an equally obscure New York Mets pitcher named Harry Parker on June 19, 1973. No. 2 came off Hennigan eight days later.

■

He batted just .196 in that nightmare rookie season, struck out 136 times in just 367 at-bats, hit 18 homers and drove in just 52 runs. But he settled into a career groove in 1974 with 36 homers, 116 RBI and found himself on the low plains of 99 homers early in his fourth full season. But just before he blasted his 100th homer, there was that incredible afternoon in Wrigley Field, Easter Saturday, 1976, the wind hammering out to left, an afternoon of unusual spring heat.

■

"I had not hit too well up to that game," Schmidt said. "But I had only had about 20 at-bats. Going 5-for-6 that game in Wrigley jacked my batting average up to among the league leaders. I remember Dick Allen teasing me in the locker room right up until national anthem time about losing the ability to have fun while I was playing the game. He said he wanted to see a smile on my face, that he and I were just going to go out and have fun. He was throwing me passes like he was a quarterback between innings.

"I flew out to leftfield my first at-bat, then I hit a homer to left in my second at-bat. Then, one of the Phillies most memorable games occurred. The first two were off Rick Reuschel, then I hit one off Mike Garman and I hit the last one off Paul Reuschel, Rick's brother, in the 11th inning, I think. We won, 14-13, and I drove in eight runs, and I had a lot of fun like Dick Allen said."

It was the first "impact" game of Schmidt's career.

"It put me on the map as a player in the National League," Schmidt said. "But the biggest thing about winning that game was what it did for our team—we won 50 out of the next 63."

And the Phillies were off and running to 101 victories and the first of three consecutive division titles.

"It really brought our team together because a lot of guys did well from that point on. I think I hit sixth in that game, and we went straight to the playoffs from that point. That was probably my third- or fourth-best all-around season. But the big highlight of the four-homer game was, I was on the cover of *Sports Illustrated* and it really gave me a lot of confidence. The wind was blowing out a little that day, not a gale, but enough to keep the ball moving.

"I hit one to dead centerfield about halfway up, and one over the bleachers in left-center. But the other two were just line shots that probably would have been a double anywhere else."

The Phillies won 101 games again in 1977 and 90 in 1978. In '77, Schmidt hit 38 homers for the third consecutive season, but in '78 he suffered a broken rib smoking a triple off Randy Jones in Shea Stadium and tailed off to 21 homers, the second-lowest total of his career.

No. 1 was at home. Then Schmidt took his milestone show on the road. The Four-homer game was in Chicago. Homer No. 100 was in Pittsburgh. The trend continued in 1979, when Schmidt stepped in to face fading former Oakland A's legend Vida Blue, who was serving his first term with the San Francisco Giants. Homer No. 10 of the 1979 season—lifetime No. 200—had Schmidt off and running to a monster year, 45 homers, 114 RBI, 109 runs scored and 120 walks. Incredibly, Schmidt collected just 137 hits that season, so 32.8 percent of his hits were home runs. A staggering 54 percent of his hits went for extra bases. The trend continued: No. 300 was in Shea Stadium and No. 400 in the photochemical haze of Dodger Stadium. Mike Krukow served No. 450 in Candlestick Park. Schmidt banged out No. 475 at the Vet off Rick Mahler last July 8, but No. 495, Schmidt's final one last season, and No. 500, left Three Rivers Stadium like tracer bullets.

■

"There is a lot of time there between '76 and '79, *whooo*," Schmidt said, forgetting about his short 1978 season. "Also, in 1978, I pounded that ball off my toe in spring training in April and didn't come back until the West Coast trip. My first game was against John Curtis in San Diego. We got snowed out at the Vet and Randy Jones pitched for the Mets then and he beat us. I remember lining out to third and I had that damn plate on my toe and it was killing me. Jones's next start was against us at their place and I cracked the rib hitting a triple down the line in right. I don't think I played for about 12 games after that."

But Schmidt was never healthier than he was in 1979.

"All I remember about No. 200 was that I hit it to dead centerfield in Candlestick Park off Vida Blue," Schmidt said.

It was an important game for the Phillies, however. Cleanup hitter Greg Luzinski was sidelined with a leg pull. Manager Danny Ozark moved his favorite player into the cleanup spot. Schmidt responded with homer No. 200, a double, and scored four runs to lead a 13-2 romp.

When he had his four-homer game in 1976, Schmidt did it in four consecutive at-bats after making an out in the first inning. Future trivia buffs take note: "I guess you've got to include this in any listing of my memorable homers," Schmidt said. "You could probably win some money on me homering in my final at-bat against the Giants at the Vet in July of 1979, then homering in my first three at-bats against them the next game. I hit one off of Gary Lavelle to end one game, then the next day I hit two off John Montefusco and I hit the third one off Pedro Borbon."

Perhaps you were there and remember the hot rush of excitement when, in his final at-bat, Schmidt lofted a towering shot to the warning track in center. No hitter had ever hit homers in five consecutive at-bats.

■

No. 283 in Game 161 of the 1980 season was the most important single home run of Schmidt's career. It was stroked under the most excruciating possible pressure in the 11th inning of the most dramatic game the Phillies had played since Game 3 of the 1977 League Championship Series, when they had coughed up a 5-3 lead with two outs in the ninth on what became known as Black Friday.

On that dismally gelid Saturday Schmidt banished forever the popular notion that he was a hollow man with a game on the line. And he became the centerpiece of one of the most incredible managerial blunders in baseball history.

After a three-hour rain delay in 38-degree weather, after 10 innings that almost defied description for their seesaw intensity, Expos manager Bill Virdon permitted journeyman righthander Stan Bahnsen to pitch to Schmidt with runners on second and third.

Schmidt crushed a 425-foot homer to left.

Virdon's capital offense? The on-deck hitter for the Phillies was wide-eyed rookie Don McCormack, Dallas Green's last catcher. Mention Virdon's incredible gaffe to any diehard Montreal fan and he will knock back his Labatt's Biere, inhale the unfiltered smoke from his Player's Navy Cut fire stick down to his pancreas and utter the consummate French Canadian blasphemy, "Tabernac!"

■

"I thought my most consistent year before last season was 1974," Schmidt said. "It looked like I was going to hit .300 until I had a bad September, and all the rest of my stats were really solid—and you've got to remember I was coming off that rookie year and had a lot of people really watching me close."

But 1980, Schmidt agreed, was his gaudiest year. It was the Year of Coming Up Big, all the way down to his performance as World Series MVP.

"I missed 12 games that year, too," he said. "I remember down the stretch I hit a couple against the Cubs and beat them at home in games we absolutely had to have. And the two real big ones were up in Montreal."

His Friday night home run off righthander Scott Sanderson in the top of the sixth gave the Phillies a one-game lead on the Expos in that fevered division race. Had they lost that game, the best the Phillies could have done was force a one-game play-off by winning the final two games of the season.

Schmidt said none of the situational fine points dawned on him when he came out to hit in the 11th inning of that crucible the next day. "All I remember was that I was 5-for-7 in the series. But I remember the home run. It was a 2-0 fastball, out over the plate and it went to leftfield.

"The dull game of baseball can be the most thrilling thing there is, and I thought that was proven in 1980. I didn't think anything could top that until I saw the Mets last October. They came pretty close to topping that with [Len] Dykstra's home run, the comeback in Game 6 of the LCS and the way they had to win the World Series. Baseball really showed its true colors last year."

■

He had a flaccid 1980 LCS with the bat (.208) against the pitcher-tough Houston Astros. "Del Unser really bailed me out in Game 5," Schmidt said. But Schmidt was the World Series MVP with a pair of homers, 7 RBI and a .381 average. Schmidt won the first of his three MVP awards. More importantly, he silenced most—not all—of the critics who claimed he never got the big hit in the big game.

■

Schmidt was headed for his greatest season in the strike year of 1981, when he repeated as the MVP. In just 102 games, he produced numbers any player would have been proud to carry for a 162-game schedule: a career-high .316 average, 31 homers and 91 RBI. Projected over 162 games, Schmidt was on a 50-homer pace.

On Aug. 14, 1981, Schmidt fired homer No. 300 off Mike Scott in Shea Stadium. The animosity between manager Dallas Green and his Knights of Labor was just starting to percolate into what would reach a plateau of ugliness. Schmidt's feat was duly noted, but to paraphrase one of Schmidt's pet sayings, nobody made a big deal of it.

The homer was part of a furious salvo Schmidt launched at the outset of the second half of major league baseball's only split season. Between Aug. 11 and 16, Schmidt pounded four homers. He would hit 14 homers before the strike and 17 after it.

The homers kept coming at a consistent pace—35 in 1982 and a league-leading 40 for the overachieving 1983 Phillies, who won a surprise pennant for interim manager Paul Owens after the firing of Pat Corrales with the club tied for first place with only a 43-42 record. The Baltimore Orioles took out the Wheeze Kids in a five-game World Series mercy killing. Afterward, Bill Giles, the new owner, released Pete Rose.

Schmidt always has loved playing in Dodger Stadium. He often has said that if all things were equal, he would have enjoyed playing his career there. He is well thought of by the Dodgers' spit-and-polish organization and is held in high regard by Dodgers fans who have waited in vain for more than a century for a third baseman with Schmidt's all-around gifts. It was appropriate, then, that No. 400 came in Dodger Stadium with a huge, festive crowd watching.

Righthander Bob Welch stood with his hands on his hips after Schmidt orbited a fifth-inning fastball into the gauzy twilight of Chavez Ravine, and the message board congratulated the Phils' star for No. 400.

There was a polite applause at first, then isolated fans began to stand up and cheer. Within seconds, the near-capacity mob was according Schmidt the level of ovation normally reserved for the men in Dodger Blue. It was one of the rare times when a visiting player was asked to take a curtain call on the road.

"I remember the reception the LA crowd gave me there. It was one of the big thrills of my career," Schmidt said. "I don't think 300 was any big deal there in New York. I wasn't called out of the dugout or anything. But there was a groundswell in LA that kept building and building. It raised gooseflesh on me."

Homers No. 450 and 475 had no real significance for Schmidt. He poled 450 off former comrade and good buddy Mike Krukow in Candlestick Park in the twilight of a forgettable 1985 season, when early season injuries forced Schmidt to first base and his slow start mirrored the getaway of a club headed for a fifth-place finish and a first sub-.500 record since 1974. However, No. 475 was special in that it was struck in Veterans Stadium last July 8 off Atlanta right-hander Rick Mahler.

Schmidt prefers to talk about the fifth-inning homer off Dwight Gooden (No. 493) last Sept. 12.

"There was electricity in the air, a lot of people in the stands and that home run might have helped rejuvenate our feelings as a team on how to win," Schmidt said. "Had the Mets come in here and stomped all over us along with everything else they were doing it would have been tough for us to finish out the season, No. 1, and, No. 2, for us to get back as an organization our feelings as a team, our ability to compete.

"Hitting that home run helped us win that game, even though we were leading at the time, 2-1. That made it 5-1, chased Gooden [to who knows where?], helped win that series and was a big steppingstone home run for a young organization. It sure helped my MVP chances."

Michael Jack Schmidt solidified his status as of Hall of Fame candidate with his entrance into the high society of a club in which the Ruths talk only to the Mayses, and the Aarons talk only to God.

1972

No.	Date	Opponent	Pitcher	Inn.
1	9/16	Montreal	Balor Moore	7

1973

No.	Date	Opponent	Pitcher	Inn.
2	4/22	St. Louis	Bob Gibson	9
3	5/15	at St. Louis	Rick Wise	2
4	6/16	San Fran.	Juan Marichal	4
5	6/18	New York	Ray Sadecki	5
6	6/19	New York	Harry Parker	4
7	6/23	at Montreal	Balor Moore	1
8	6/27	at New York	Harry Parker	5
9	6/27	at New York	Phil Hennigan	6
10	7/ 3	at Chicago	Milt Pappas	2
11	7/ 6	Cincinnati	Fred Norman	2
12	7/29	at Pittsburgh	Luke Walker	7
13	8/ 4	Pittsburgh	Luke Walker	4
14	8/10	at Los Ang.	Tommy John	7
15	8/10	at Los Ang.	Doug Rau	9
16	8/27	San Fran.	Jim Barr	1
17	9/11	New York	Jerry Koosman	6
18	9/18	at Chicago	Bill Bonham	3
19	9/21	St. Louis	Rick Wise	4

1974

No.	Date	Opponent	Pitcher	Inn.
20	4/ 6	New York	Tug McGraw	9
21	4/19	Chicago	Bill Bonham	3
22	4/27	at San Diego	Randy Jones	6
23	5/ 1	at San Fran.	Jim Willoughby	6
24	5/10	Pittsburgh	Ken Brett	6
25	5/11	Pittsburgh	Bob Moose	3
26	5/18	at Pittsburgh	Bob Moose	6
27	5/27	at Atlanta	Phil Niekro	7
28	6/ 1	San Fran.	Mike Caldwell	1
29	6/ 1	San Fran.	Mike Caldwell	3
30	6/ 3	Atlanta	Carl Morton	1
31	6/ 5	Atlanta	Phil Niekro	3
32	6/ 8	Cincinnati	Tom Hall	5
33	6/ 9	Cincinnati	Pedro Borbon	7
34	6/14	at Cincinnati	Don Gullett	3
35	6/14	at Cincinnati	Don Gullett	5
36	6/17	Houston	Don Wilson	5
37	6/29	at Pittsburgh	Jerry Reuss	4
38	7/18	at San Diego	Bill Greif	8
39	7/27	Pittsburgh	Bruce Kison	1
40	7/29	Pittsburgh	Jerry Reuss	4
41	7/29	Pittsburgh	Jerry Reuss	6
42	7/31	St. Louis	Mike Garman	9
43	8/ 4	at St. Louis	Alan Foster	1
44	8/ 4	at St. Louis	Alan Foster	7
45	8/13	San Fran.	Jim Barr	1
46	8/13	San Fran.	Jim Barr	3
47	8/17	at Atlanta	Buzz Capra	4
48	8/18	at Atlanta	Ron Reed	5
49	8/19	at Cincinnati	Don Gullett	4
50	8/21	at Cincinnati	Tom Carroll	3
51	8/21	at Cincinnati	Tom Hall	8
52	9/ 1	Houston	Jim York	7
53	9/ 2	at Pittsburgh	Jerry Reuss	1
54	9/10	at St. Louis	Alan Foster	1
55	9/12	Pittsburgh	Jerry Reuss	8

1975

No.	Date	Opponent	Pitcher	Inn.
56	4/14	New York	Jerry Cram	9
57	4/17	Chicago	Ray Burris	2
58	5/ 2	Pittsburgh	Bruce Kison	1
59	5/ 3	Pittsburgh	Jim Rooker	1
60	5/ 7	at St. Louis	Bob Forsch	3
61	5/16	Atlanta	Buzz Capra	3
62	6/ 2	San Diego	Dave Freisleben	3
63	6/ 3	San Diego	Dan Spillner	3
64	6/ 3	San Diego	Larry Hardy	6
65	6/ 4	San Diego	Randy Jones	2
66	6/ 6	Los Angeles	Burt Hooton	6
67	6/10	at San Diego	Dan Spillner	9
68	6/18	at Chicago	Steve Stone	4
69	6/30	St. Louis	Bob Forsch	7
70	7/ 9	at Cincinnati	Rawley Eastwick	9
71	7/13	at Houston	Larry Dierker	2
72	7/17	Houston	Doug Konieczny	2
73	7/18	Houston	Wayne Granger	8
74	7/20	Cincinnati	Clay Kirby	2
75	8/ 1	at Montreal	Don Carrithers	2
76	8/ 3	at Montreal	Steve Rogers	8
77	8/ 5	Chicago	Bill Bonham	1
78	8/ 5	Chicago	Milt Wilcox	5
79	8/ 7	Chicago	Rick Reuschel	3
80	8/ 9	San Fran.	Gary Lavelle	5
81	8/15	San Diego	Joe McIntosh	2
82	8/18	at Atlanta	Phil Niekro	2
83	8/18	at Atlanta	Phil Niekro	7
84	8/22	at San Diego	Bill Greif	9
85	8/24	at San Diego	Randy Jones	5
86	8/25	at Los Ang.	Andy Messersmith	2
87	9/ 5	Chicago	Oscar Zamora	8
88	9/ 9	St. Louis	Greg Terlecky	8
89	9/11	at Montreal	Steve Rogers	4
90	9/14	at Chicago	Steve Stone	2
91	9/14	at Chicago	Tom Dettore	7
92	9/18	Pittsburgh	Dock Ellis	2
93	9/20	at New York	Jerry Koosman	3

1976

No.	Date	Opponent	Pitcher	Inn.
94	4/11	Pittsburgh	Bruce Kison	5
95	4/17	at Chicago	Rick Reuschel	5
96	4/17	at Chicago	Rick Reuschel	7
97	4/17	at Chicago	Mike Garman	8
98	4/17	at Chicago	Paul Reuschel	10
99	4/18	at Chicago	Paul Reuschel	7
100	4/20	at Pittsburgh	John Candelaria	4
101	4/21	at Pittsburgh	Doc Medich	8
102	4/24	Atlanta	Elias Sosa	8
103	4/26	Cincinnati	Fred Norman	3
104	4/26	Cincinnati	Fred Norman	4
105	5/ 1	at Atlanta	Dick Ruthven	5
106	5/11	San Diego	Mike Dupree	8
107	5/15	at Houston	Larry Dierker	4
108	5/20	at New York	Tom Seaver	3
109	6/10	at Los Ang.	Doug Rau	6
110	6/17	San Fran.	Randy Moffitt	8

No.	Date	Opponent	Pitcher	Inn.
111	6/18	Cincinnati	Jack Billingham	5
112	6/19	Cincinnati	Gary Nolan	6
113	6/23	at Cincinnati	Santo Alcala	4
114	6/28	at Montreal	Steve Rogers	6
115	7/6	Los Angeles	Doug Rau	1
116	7/9	San Diego	Brent Strom	6
117	7/15	at San Fran.	Jim Barr	4
118	7/23	Pittsburgh	Rick Langford	6
119	7/25	Pittsburgh	John Candelaria	5
120	8/1	at New York	Nino Espinosa	3
121	8/4	at Chicago	Steve Renko	4
122	8/4	at Chicago	Joe Coleman	7
123	8/8	at St. Louis	Eric Rasmussen	3
124	8/14	San Fran.	Jim Barr	5
125	8/19	Houston	Joaquin Andujar	1
126	9/4	at New York	Nino Espinosa	6
127	9/3	Montreal	Dennis Blair	1
128	9/13	Montreal	Steve Dunning	5
129	9/21	St. Louis	John Denny	6
130	9/25	at Montreal	Woodie Fryman	1
131	9/29	at St. Louis	Bob Forsch	5

1977

No.	Date	Opponent	Pitcher	Inn.
132	4/10	Montreal	Don Stanhouse	6
133	4/16	at Montreal	Gerry Hannahs	4
134	4/18	at Chicago	Ray Burris	6
135	5/5	at San Diego	Rollie Fingers	7
136	5/7	at Los Ang.	Al Downing	13
137	5/10	San Fran.	Don Heaverlo	6
138	5/12	San Fran.	John Montefusco	4
139	6/6	Houston	Bo McLaughlin	5
140	6/7	Houston	Floyd Bannister	1
141	6/10	at Atlanta	Max Leon	3
142	6/10	at Atlanta	Dave Campbell	7
143	6/13	at Cincinnati	Woodie Fryman	2
144	6/14	at Cincinnati	Fred Norman	4
145	6/15	at Cincinnati	Gary Nolan	1
146	6/17	Atlanta	Steve Kline	8
147	6/20	Cincinnati	Fred Norman	4
148	6/22	Cincinnati	Dale Murray	5
149	6/22	Cincinnati	Doug Capilla	8
150	6/25	at St. Louis	Bob Forsch	3
151	6/26	at St. Louis	Larry Dierker	1
152	6/30	Pittsburgh	Larry Demery	4
153	7/2	Pittsburgh	Jerry Reuss	3
154	7/3	Pittsburgh	Larry Demery	8
155	7/5	New York	Pat Zachry	3
156	7/7	New York	Nino Espinosa	3
157	7/12	St. Louis	Eric Rasmussen	4
158	7/25	at San Diego	Bob Shirley	9
159	7/31	San Fran.	Ed Halicki	4
160	8/14	at Chicago	Mike Krukow	5
161	8/14	at Chicago	Paul Reuschel	5
162	8/23	at Atlanta	Phil Niekro	5
163	8/27	at Cincinnati	Mario Soto	1
164	9/6	at Pittsburgh	Jerry Reuss	1
165	9/8	at New York	Nino Espinosa	4
166	9/15	New York	Bob Myrick	4
167	9/16	at St. Louis	Pete Falcone	8
168	9/23	at Montreal	Joe Kerrigan	4
169	9/27	at Chicago	Dennis Lamp	8

1978

No.	Date	Opponent	Pitcher	Inn.
170	4/9	St. Louis	Dave Hamilton	4
171	4/22	at Montreal	Ross Grimsley	1
172	4/24	Chicago	Mike Krukow	6
173	4/26	Chicago	Rick Reuschel	7
174	5/5	New York	Nino Espinosa	5
175	5/13	Cincinnati	Doug Bair	8
176	5/14	Cincinnati	Tom Hume	6
177	5/21	at New York	Jerry Koosman	1
178	6/12	at Los Ang.	Burt Hooton	4
179	6/13	at Los Ang.	Don Sutton	1
180	6/24	Chicago	Ken Holtzman	1
181	7/21	Houston	Joe Niekro	3
182	7/28	at Cincinnati	Fred Norman	1
183	8/2	New York	Jerry Koosman	3
184	8/18	San Fran.	Bob Knepper	3
185	8/19	San Fran.	John Montefusco	1
186	9/4	at St. Louis	Aurelio Lopez	1
187	9/6	at Chicago	Rick Reuschel	3
188	9/13	Chicago	Donnie Moore	8
189	9/16	New York	Dwight Bernard	10
190	9/20	at Montreal	Dan Schatzeder	6

1979

No.	Date	Opponent	Pitcher	Inn.
191	4/7	at St. Louis	Pete Vuckovich	4
192	4/11	Pittsburgh	Bert Blyleven	8
193	4/15	at New York	Wayne Twitchell	8
194	4/17	at Pittsburgh	Bert Blyleven	3
195	5/3	at Los Ang.	Rick Sutcliffe	9
196	5/4	at Los Ang.	Don Sutton	5
197	5/5	at Los Ang.	Andy Messersmith	5
198	5/5	at Los Ang.	Charlie Hough	8
199	5/6	at Los Ang.	Doug Rau	5
200	5/13	at San Fran.	Vida Blue	2
201	5/15	at Chicago	Lynn McGlothen	1
202	5/16	at Chicago	Bill Caudill	8
203	5/17	at Chicago	Dennis Lamp	1
204	5/17	at Chicago	Bruce Sutter	10
205	5/21	St. Louis	John Denny	6
206	6/3	at Cincinnati	Tom Hume	9
207	6/5	at Houston	George Throop	5
208	6/12	Houston	Rick Williams	5
209	6/18	at Atlanta	Rick Matula	3
210	6/20	at Atlanta	Craig Skok	9
211	6/26	Chicago	Donnie Moore	2
212	6/29	at St. Louis	Bob Forsch	4
213	6/30	at St. Louis	John Fulgham	2
214	7/6	San Fran.	Gary Lavelle	5
215	7/7	San Fran.	John Montefusco	2
216	7/7	San Fran.	John Montefusco	3
217	7/7	San Fran.	Pedro Borbon	6
218	7/8	San Fran.	Bob Knepper	7
219	7/9	San Fran.	Vida Blue	6
220	7/10	San Diego	Vida Blue	6
221	7/14	Los Angeles	Don Sutton	3
222	7/20	at San Fran.	John Montefusco	4
223	7/22	at San Diego	Steve Mura	7
224	7/23	at San Diego	Randy Jones	4
225	7/25	at Los Ang.	Rick Sutcliffe	1
226	7/29	St. Louis	Pete Vuckovich	1
227	8/2	at New York	Pete Falcone	4
228	8/3	at Pittsburgh	Bruce Kison	7
229	8/8	Montreal	Steve Rogers	3
230	8/29	Cincinnati	Bill Bonham	1

101

No.	Date	Opponent	Pitcher	Inn.
231	8/31	at Atlanta	Tony Brizzolara	3
232	9/ 1	at Atlanta	Phil Niekro	7
233	9/19	Pittsburgh	Enrique Romo	7
234	9/22	Montreal	Steve Rogers	5
235	9/28	at Montreal	Dave Palmer	6

1980

No.	Date	Opponent	Pitcher	Inn.
236	4/18	at Montreal	Scott Sanderson	5
237	4/19	at Montreal	Dale Murray	9
238	4/22	New York	Tom Hausman	1
239	4/22	New York	John Pacella	8
240	5/ 2	Los Angeles	Rick Sutcliffe	1
241	5/ 3	Los Angeles	Burt Hooton	2
242	5/ 5	Atlanta	Rick Matula	3
243	5/ 5	Atlanta	Rick Matula	4
244	5/10	at Cincinnati	Tom Seaver	6
245	5/20	Cincinnati	Charlies Leibrandt	1
246	5/23	Houston	Nolan Ryan	3
247	5/25	Houston	Ken Forsch	5
248	5/27	Pittsburgh	Jim Bibby	9
249	5/28	Pittsburgh	Don Robinson	1
250	5/31	at Chicago	Willie Hernandez	3
251	5/31	at Chicago	Bill Caudill	7
252	6/ 1	at Chicago	Dick Tidrow	7
253	6/ 3	at Pittsburgh	Eddie Solomon	1
254	6/13	San Diego	Randy Jones	1
255	6/14	San Diego	Steve Mura	1
256	6/24	Montreal	Dave Palmer	5
257	7/12	Pittsburgh	Jim Bibby	2
258	7/18	at Atlanta	Phil Niekro	6
259	7/23	at Cincinnati	Bruce Berenyi	1
260	7/25	Atlanta	Larry McWilliams	1
261	7/25	Atlanta	Larry McWilliams	3
262	7/29	Houston	Bert Roberge	1
263	8/11	at Chicago	Willie Hernandez	3
264	8/12	at Chicago	Mike Krukow	1
265	8/13	at Chicago	Dick Tidrow	9
266	8/14	at New York	Ed Glynn	7
267	8/16	at New York	Craig Swan	4
268	8/21	San Diego	Rick Wise	1
269	8/21	San Diego	Rick Wise	8
270	8/24	San Fran.	Bob Knepper	3
271	9/ 4	at Los Ang.	Jerry Reuss	1
272	9/ 8	Pittsburgh	Don Robinson	6
273	9/11	at New York	Ray Burris	4
274	9/16	at Pittsburgh	Jim Bibby	9
275	9/20	at Chicago	Lynn McGlothen	1
276	9/21	at Chicago	Dick Tidrow	9
277	9/22	at St. Louis	Pete Vuckovich	4
278	9/23	at St. Louis	Alan Olmsted	9
279	9/27	Montreal	Scott Sanderson	1
280	10/ 1	Chicago	Dennis Lamp	6
281	10/ 2	Chicago	Randy Martz	4
282	10/ 3	at Montreal	Scott Sanderson	6
283	10/ 4	at Montreal	Stan Bahnsen	11

1981

No.	Date	Opponent	Pitcher	Inn.
284	4/11	at St. Louis	Bob Forsch	1
285	4/16	Pittsburgh	Don Robinson	2
286	4/22	at Montreal	Bill Gullickson	9
287	4/24	at Chicago	Rick Reuschel	5
288	4/24	at Chicago	Bill Caudill	3
289	5/ 2	San Fran.	Ed Whitson	4
290	5/ 3	San Fran.	Tom Griffin	3
291	5/ 3	San Fran.	Gary Lavelle	7
292	5/ 8	San Diego	John Curtis	5
293	5/ 8	San Diego	John Littlefield	8
294	5/17	at San Diego	Danny Boone	5
295	5/18	at Los Ang.	Fernando Valenzuela	1
296	5/20	at Los Ang.	Burt Hooton	3
297	5/23	at Pittsburgh	Grant Jackson	9
298	8/11	St. Louis	Joaquin Andujar	6
299	8/13	St. Louis	John Martin	4
300	8/14	at New York	Mike Scott	3
301	8/16	at New York	Pat Zachry	4
302	8/22	Houston	Dave Smith	5
303	8/23	Houston	Bob Knepper	3
304	8/24	Atlanta	Rick Camp	8
305	8/30	at Houston	Nolan Ryan	8
306	8/31	at Atlanta	Gaylord Perry	5
307	9/ 3	Cincinnati	Bruce Berenyi	3
308	9/ 9	Montreal	Bill Gullickson	4
309	9/16	at New York	Pat Zachry	5
310	9/20	Pittsburgh	Kent Tekulve	7
311	9/25	at Chicago	Ken Kravec	4
312	9/30	St. Louis	Bob Forsch	3
313	10/ 2	Chicago	Dick Tidrow	9
314	10/ 3	Chicago	Jay Howell	5

1982

No.	Date	Opponent	Pitcher	Inn.
315	5/ 2	at San Diego	John Curtis	5
316	5/ 7	San Diego	Luis DeLeon	9
317	5/ 8	San Diego	John Montefusco	8
318	6/ 7	Chicago	Dickie Noles	5
319	6/ 9	Chicago	Ferguson Jenkins	1
320	6/14	at Chicago	Ferguson Jenkins	6
321	6/26	New York	Neil Allen	8
322	7/ 4	at New York	Neil Allen	9
323	7/ 7	San Diego	Tim Lollar	8
324	7/ 9	Los Angeles	Jerry Reuss	3
325	7/17	at San Fran.	Greg Minton	8
326	7/18	at San Fran.	Atlee Hammaker	1
327	7/19	at San Fran.	John Curtis	2
328	7/21	at San Diego	Tim Lollar	4
329	7/23	at Los Ang.	Dave Stewart	3
330	7/28	at Pittsburgh	Rick Rhoden	6
331	7/29	Chicago	Doug Bird	6
332	7/30	Chicago	Ferguson Jenkins	3
333	7/31	Chicago	Allen Ripley	4
334	8/ 5	Montreal	Charlie Lea	4
335	8/ 6	at Chicago	Allen Ripley	1
336	8/ 7	at Chicago	Lee Smith	9
337	8/ 9	Pittsburgh	Larry McWilliams	3
338	8/10	Pittsburgh	Enrique Romo	7
339	8/12	at Montreal	Woodie Fryman	9
340	8/15	at Montreal	Steve Rogers	9
341	8/21	at Cincinnati	Bob Shirley	8
342	8/30	Atlanta	Rick Mahler	1
343	9/ 3	Houston	Joe Niekro	9
344	9/ 5	Houston	Nolan Ryan	6
345	9/ 7	at Chicago	Allen Ripley	6
346	9/11	at Pittsburgh	Larry McWilliams	5
347	9/12	at Pittsburgh	Rick Rhoden	3
348	9/21	at St. Louis	Eric Rasmussen	4
349	10/ 3	New York	Ed Lynch	

1983

No.	Date	Opponent	Pitcher	Inn.
350	4/ 8	at San Fran.	Fred Breining	4
351	4/13	New York	Craig Swan	3
352	4/16	Atlanta	Phil Niekro	1
353	4/16	Chicago	Paul Moskau	3
354	4/24	at Houston	Mike LaCoss	1
355	4/26	at Atlanta	Pascual Perez	1
356	5/ 3	at Cincinnati	Charlie Puleo	7
357	5/28	Montreal	Jeff Reardon	9
358	5/29	Montreal	Bryn Smith	7
359	6/ 3	at San Diego	Tim Lollar	4
360	6/ 7	St. Louis	Bob Forsch	2
361	6/11	Pittsburgh	Rod Scurry	8
362	6/21	at Montreal	Bryn Smith	7
363	6/21	at Montreal	Randy Lerch	6
364	7/ 3	New York	Doug Sisk	8
365	7/11	at Cincinnati	Bruce Berenyi	3
366	7/11	at Cincinnati	Tom Hume	11
367	7/17	Cincinnati	Frank Pastore	5
368	7/21	at Atlanta	Rick Camp	5
369	7/23	at Atlanta	Ken Dayley	1
370	7/23	at Atlanta	Steve Bedrosian	3
371	7/24	at Atlanta	Pascual Perez	6
372	7/28	at Houston	Mike LaCoss	8
373	8/ 7	at St. Louis	Neil Allen	4
374	8/ 8	Pittsburgh	John Candelaria	3
375	8/ 8	Pittsburgh	Lee Tunnell	7
376	8/15	at Chicago	Lee Smith	8
377	8/20	at Los Ang.	Fernando Valenzuela	4
378	8/29	San Diego	Elias Sosa	1
379	8/29	San Diego	Sid Monge	7
380	8/30	San Diego	Ed Whitson	1
381	8/30	San Diego	Ed Whitson	4
382	9/ 5	at New York	Mike Torrez	3
383	9/ 7	at New York	Scott Holman	9
384	9/14	Montreal	Greg Barger	4
385	9/14	Montreal	Ray Burris	1
386	9/18	St. Louis	Joaquin Andujar	1
387	9/22	at Montreal	Charlie Lea	3
388	9/24	at St. Louis	Bruce Sutter	9
389	9/28	at Chicago	Dick Ruthven	3

1984

No.	Date	Opponent	Pitcher	Inn.
390	4/ 3	at Atlanta	Len Barker	1
391	4/10	Houston	Nolan Ryan	8
392	4/14	at Montreal	Bill Gullickson	3
393	4/17	at Pittsburgh	John Tudor	6
394	5/ 2	Montreal	Dan Schatzeder	6
395	5/ 4	Cincinnati	Frank Pastore	2
396	5/ 5	Cincinnati	Bill Scherrer	2
397	5/ 6	Cincinnati	Jeff Russell	3
398	5/10	at Houston	Mike Scott	7
399	5/11	at San Diego	Rich Gossage	8
400	5/15	at Los Ang.	Bob Welch	5
401	5/20	at San Fran.	Scott Garrelts	9
402	6/ 2	Chicago	Lee Smith	8
403	6/17	at Chicago	Lee Smith	9
404	6/19	at New York	Ed Lynch	5
405	6/26	New York	Walt Terrell	3
406	7/15	at Houston	Bob Knepper	4
407	7/16	at Cincinnati	Keefe Cato	1
408	7/18	at Cincinnati	Keefe Cato	5
409	7/18	at Cincinnati	Brad Lesley	7
410	7/20	at Atlanta	Len Barker	4
411	8/ 7	at Montreal	Bryn Smith	3
412	8/15	at San Diego	Tim Lollar	9
413	8/16	at San Diego	Andy Hawkins	4
414	8/16	at San Diego	Greg Harris	7
415	8/24	Los Angeles	Alejandro Pena	1
416	8/30	San Fran.	Mark Davis	6
417	8/31	San Fran.	Bill Laskey	1
418	9/ 3	Chicago	Rick Sutcliffe	4
419	9/ 9	at Montreal	Bill Gullickson	3
420	9/13	St. Louis	Joaquin Andujar	2
421	9/14	Montreal	Steve Rogers	1
422	9/14	Montreal	Joe Hesketh	5
423	9/15	Montreal	Bill Gullickson	9
424	9/22	at Pittsburgh	Rick Rhoden	4
425	9/30	Pittsburgh	Larry McWilliams	1

1985

No.	Date	Opponent	Pitcher	Inn.
426	4/24	at Montreal	Dan Schatzeder	9
427	4/29	Montreal	Bryn Smith	7
428	5/13	at Cincinnati	John Stuper	4
429	5/14	at Cincinnati	Tom Browning	6
430	5/19	Los Angeles	Ken Howell	9
431	5/27	San Diego	Tim Stoddard	5
432	6/23	Pittsburgh	Jose DeLeon	2
433	6/26	St. Louis	Danny Cox	1
434	6/28	at Montreal	Bryn Smith	4
435	7/ 5	Cincinnati	Tom Browning	2
436	7/13	at Atlanta	Rick Mahler	8
437	7/18	at Cincinnati	Mario Soto	5
438	7/22	Houston	Jeff Heathcock	9
439	7/23	Houston	Bob Knepper	1
440	7/26	Atlanta	Rick Mahler	1
441	8/ 2	at St. Louis	John Tudor	4
442	8/ 3	at St. Louis	Kurt Kepshire	4
443	8/ 8	Pittsburgh	Don Robinson	2
444	8/11	St. Louis	Bob Forsch	5
445	8/15	at New York	Dwight Gooden	2
446	8/17	at Chicago	George Frazier	7
447	8/18	at Chicago	Jay Baller	4
448	8/30	at Los Ang.	Bob Welch	2
449	9/ 3	at San Fran.	Atlee Hammaker	1
450	9/ 4	at San Fran.	Mike Krukow	6
451	9/ 7	at San Diego	Andy Hawkins	4
452	9/10	Montreal	Tim Burke	11
453	9/11	Montreal	Bill Gullickson	6
454	9/15	at Pittsburgh	Rick Reuschel	8
455	9/23	New York	Rick Aguilera	4
456	9/28	at Chicago	Dave Beard	7
457	9/28	at Chicago	Lee Smith	9
458	10/ 3	at Montreal	Bill Laskey	3

1986

No.	Date	Opponent	Pitcher	Inn.
459	4/ 7	at Cincinnati	Mario Soto	3
460	4/18	at New York	Ron Darling	1
461	4/24	at Pittsburgh	Rick Rhoden	1
462	4/25	at Pittsburgh	Rick Rhoden	9
463	4/29	Houston	Nolan Ryan	1
464	5/22	at San Diego	Andy Hawkins	6
465	5/23	at Los Ang.	Tom Niedenfuer	7
466	5/27	San Fran.	Jeff Robinson	8
467	6/ 2	Los Ang.	Jerry Reuss	1
468	6/ 6	at Montreal	Joe Hesketh	1
469	6/19	St. Louis	Greg Bargar	6
470	6/22	St. Louis	Greg Mathews	7

No.	Date	Opponent	Pitcher	Inn.
471	6/23	Chicago	Jamie Moyer	3
472	6/25	Chicago	Scott Sanderson	4
473	7/ 1	at Pittsburgh	Larry McWilliams	12
474	7/ 3	Cincinnati	John Denny	1
475	7/ 8	Atlanta	Rick Mahler	4
476	7/13	at Houston	Bob Knepper	6
477	7/13	at Houston	Dave Smith	11
478	7/17	at Cincinnati	John Franco	8
479	7/19	at Cincinnati	Bill Gullickson	4
480	7/25	Houston	Larry Andersen	3
481	8/ 1	Chicago	Ed Lynch	5
482	8/ 3	Chicago	Frank DiPino	8
483	8/13	New York	Bob Ojeda	1
484	8/16	Pittsburgh	Larry McWilliams	3
485	8/19	at San Fran.	Kelly Downs	3
486	8/30	San Fran.	Mike LaCoss	4
487	8/31	San Fran.	Vida Blue	6
488	9/ 3	San Diego	LaMarr Hoyt	1
489	9/ 6	Los Ang.	Fernando Valenzuela	1
490	9/ 9	at Chicago	Jamie Moyer	4
491	9/10	at Chicago	Rick Sutcliffe	6
492	9/10	at Chicago	Frank DiPino	7
493	9/12	New York	Dwight Gooden	5
494	9/15	Pittsburgh	Rick Rhoden	6
495	9/22	at Pittsburgh	John Smiley	7

1987

No.	Date	Opponent	Pitcher	Inn.
496	4/10	Chicago	Ed Lynch	6
497	4/11	Chicago	Rick Sutcliffe	2
498	4/14	New York	Ron Darling	5
499	4/17	at Pittsburgh	Bob Patterson	2
500	4/18	at Pittsburgh	Don Robinson	9

Mike Schmidt's Career Statistics

REGULAR SEASON

Year	Team	G	AB	R	H	2B	3B	HR	RBI	BB	SO	SB	CS	E	Avg.
1972	Phillies	13	34	2	7	0	0	1	3	5	15	0	0	2	.206
1973	Phillies	132	367	43	72	11	0	18	52	62	136	8	0	18	.196
1974	Phillies	162	568	108	160	28	7	36	116	106	138	23	2	26	.282
1975	Phillies	158	562	93	140	34	3	38	95	101	180	29	12	26	.249
1976	Phillies	160	584	112	153	31	4	38	107	100	149	14	9	21	.262
1977	Phillies	154	544	114	149	27	11	38	101	104	122	15	8	20	.274
1978	Phillies	145	513	93	129	27	2	21	78	91	103	19	6	16	.251
1979	Phillies	160	541	109	137	25	4	45	114	120	115	9	5	23	.253
1980	Phillies	150	548	104	157	25	8	48	121	89	119	12	5	27	.286
1981	Phillies	102	354	78	112	19	2	31	91	73	71	12	4	15	.316
1982	Phillies	148	514	108	144	26	3	35	87	107	131	14	7	23	.280
1983	Phillies	154	534	104	136	16	4	40	109	128	148	7	8	19	.255
1984	Phillies	151	528	93	146	23	3	36	106	92	116	5	3	26	.277
1985	Phillies	158	549	89	152	31	5	33	93	87	117	1	1	18	.277
1986	Phillies	160	552	97	160	29	1	37	119	89	84	1	2	8	.290
1987	Phillies	147	522	88	153	28	0	35	113	83	80	2	1	13	.293
Totals		2251	7814	1435	2107	380	57	530	1505	1437	1824	171	91	301	.270

DIVISION SERIES

Year	Opponent	G	AB	R	H	2B	3B	HR	RBI	BB	SO	SB	CS	E	Avg.
1981	Montreal	5	16	3	4	1	0	1	2	4	2	0	0	1	.250

LEAGUE CHAMPIONSHIP SERIES

Year	Opponent	G	AB	R	H	2B	3B	HR	RBI	BB	SO	SB	CS	E	Avg.
1976	Cincinnati	3	12	1	4	1	0	0	0	0	1	0	0	1	.308
1977	Los Angeles	4	16	2	1	0	0	0	2	2	3	0	0	0	.063
1978	Los Angeles	4	15	2	3	1	0	0	1	2	3	0	0	2	.200
1980	Houston	5	24	1	5	2	0	0	1	1	6	0	0	1	.208
1983	Los Angeles	4	15	4	7	2	0	1	1	2	2	1	0	1	.467
Totals		20	83	10	20	7	0	1	5	7	15	1	0	5	.241

WORLD SERIES

Year	Opponent	G	AB	R	H	2B	3B	HR	RBI	BB	SO	SB	CS	E	Avg.
1980	Kansas City	6	21	6	8	1	0	2	7	4	3	0	0	1	.381
1983	Baltimore	5	20	0	1	0	0	0	0	0	6	0	0	1	.050
Totals		11	41	6	9	1	0	2	7	4	9	0	0	1	.220

AN UNLIKELY SUPERSTAR

BY MARK KRAM

Dayton, Ohio—One had batted .435 and had been an all-state selection as a high school senior; the other hit for a far lower average and had delicate knees. Of the two, Tom Smith of Kiser High School seemed to have far more potential. The Washington Senators were so enthusiastic that they offered Smith a $13,500 signing bonus. He accepted a scholarship to Ohio University.

The third baseman at rival Fairview High School seemed decidedly less promising. Though, at 17, he had a strong arm and seemed to possess a certain poise, Mike Schmidt had shown no evidence of the power he would develop and bore the scars of two knee operations. He received neither a pro offer nor a college scholarship. He enrolled at Ohio U., won the starting shortstop job as a sophomore and roomed for three of his four years there with Tom Smith.

Sixteen years have passed since Smith and Schmidt parted in college. Still close, the two see each other on those biannual occasions when the Phillies travel to Cincinnati; Smith drives down and sleeps in the extra bed Schmidt has in his room. Though it would appear the two now revolve in independent orbits, Smith claims—and Schmidt agrees—that the "goals we shared in college" helped shape and strengthen their friendship.

"Schmitty and I both had the same ambitions," Smith said. "We wanted to be big leaguers."

That Schmidt would do that and more would have seemed inconceivable in 1967, the spring he received his high school diploma. "No one would have said then that Schmidt would have stood out in the crowd then," said Ritter Collett, the sports editor at the *Dayton Journal-Herald*. Collett remembers that he had been more impressed with Smith. Schmidt still considers Smith one of the top players to ever come out of Dayton. "He was far more advanced than I was at that stage," Schmidt said.

That would change. While both had successful college careers and were drafted (Schmidt by the Phillies, Smith by the Angels), Smith never got higher than Double A. Cut in successive springs by California, Houston, and the Phillies, he started to see "the handwriting on the wall" and now has a job in shipping and receiving at General Motors. He is divorced and lives in a trailer park in north Dayton.

Though his own career ended in disappointment—and contributed, he confesses, to the "restlessness" he has experienced—Smith has extracted a certain pride from the success Schmidt has achieved. To prove it, he retrieves a black attache case from the back of his Trans-Am and sets it on a table. Inside of that case is a binder and inside of that, preserved in plastic and arranged in chronological order, are pages and pages of bubble gum cards of "Schmitty."

■

The 1967 graduating class of Fairview High School will celebrate its 20th class reunion this spring. In a certain way, Schmidt claims he would enjoy attending, but only if he could blend in and not be treated as the center of attention. He has not seen some of his high school friends in years. Though his parents still live in Dayton and his sister operates a travel agency there, he seldom visits and would be curious to know what has become of some people.

To his ex-coaches and teammates still living in the area, Schmidt is a source of continuing curiosity; it is as if each had part in a historical event.

"I keep an eye on Schmidt in the box scores in the *Journal-Herald*," said David Palsgrove, one of two baseball coaches Schmidt had at Fairview. Former Fairview teammate Lonn Jackson, now the co-owner of Jaxon Corn Meal Mush, watches Schmidt on television and shakes his head.

"Still today, as successful as he has been, a certain Hall of

Famer, I have a difficult time believing that this is the *same guy*," Jackson said. "This is someone who is going to be remembered as Mays and Mantle are remembered. I see [Schmidt] out there and sit there in disbelief."

The son of an athletic father—Jack Schmidt is a skillful golfer—Schmidt seemed to have far more potential as a basketball or football player; he participated in both in high school. Ron Bradley, then the football coach at Fairview, claims Schmidt would have been an excellent college quarterback. "He had a strong arm and he had brains," said Bradley, now the principal at Northmont Junior High School. Schmidt wonders if he would have pursued baseball with the same enthusiasm were it not for his knee injuries, both of which were football-related.

"I probably would have starred in football at one of the small colleges in the area and that would have been that," Schmidt said. "I would never have given baseball the time I ended up giving it. I guess I would have ended up being a professional soda jerk."

No one remembers Schmidt excelling in baseball. "On a scale of 1 to 10," Palsgrove said, "he would have been a 6." Though Schmidt had been a Little League star, and clippings of his exploits are preserved in the scrapbook his parents keep, he had trouble adjusting to the curve. Bob Galvin coached Schmidt as a senior and said he was one of the few players he ever had—"if not the only one I had"—who worked on weaknesses. Said Galvin of the young Schmidt, "He *wanted* the batting practice pitcher to throw him that curve."

That would have been typical of Schmidt then. Galvin recalls a snowy day that spring when he assumed that it would be understood that practice had been canceled. Galvin was sitting at home when Schmidt called. "He had the whole team out there practicing in the snow," Galvin recalled. "He wanted to know where *I* was." To Galvin and others, that dedication seemed to distinguish Schmidt from his teammates. Lonn Jackson described it as focus.

"I can remember how he always seemed to be concerned with how we looked as a team; for instance, how we tossed the ball around the infield [after a strikeout]," Jackson said.

"Mike would say, 'Now this is the way we have to do it: the ball has to go from third to short to second back to third. Skip the catcher.' He wanted it done the *big-league way*. He always seemed to be focused."

The City League coaches selected Jackson and Fairview teammates Ron Neff, a catcher, and Bob Slack to the All-City team that spring; of the three, Neff appeared to be the only one with big-league potential. Considered one of the two top high school catchers in the state—the other, Steve Yeager, signed with the Dodgers that spring—Neff had a partial scholarship offer from Ohio University. Schmidt recalls how jealous he had been of his friends that spring.

"All of them seemed to be getting offers except for me," Schmidt said. "Ohio University wanted Neff. Yeager signed with the Dodgers. I was so jealous of those two I could have spit."

Why Neff never attended Ohio University—and never attended college—is a source of vague curiosity to Schmidt. Uncertain as a high school senior where he wanted to attend college, Schmidt drove over to Athens with Neff and toured the Ohio U. campus with its coach, Bob Wren. Schmidt can recall each detail of that day.

"The coaches there wanted Neff to come there and catch for them," Schmidt said. "They said I could come along and travel with the team.

"Ron had been a perfect catcher: big, strong, always hit over .300. Why he never accepted that scholarship is something I have never understood."

■

He is sitting in the living room of his home in Vandalia, a suburb of Dayton, and he is explaining how, in 1980, Firestone closed its plant in Dayton and laid off 1,600 workers. He was one of them. He has since worked as bartender and in sales. He currently manages a social club.

To characterize Ron Neff as consumed by regret would be an exaggeration; he does, however, wonder what would have happened if he had attended college. "I was a shy kid then," Neff said, "but I was cocky too. I had the answers."

He seems to see himself then and smiles.

"I got married that summer and got a job," he said. "Four years later I got divorced."

That Schmidt has done as well as he has is of no shock to Neff. "He always had home run potential," Neff said, "but he had to prove he could do it more consistently." Schmidt did exactly that: While Neff reported to his shift at Dayton Tire and Rubber and supported a wife, Schmidt enrolled at Ohio University and blossomed into a prospect. He started at shortstop, helped Ohio University to the College World Series in 1970 and twice won All-America honors.

Of the handful of people who helped Schmidt get to that point, none were as influential as his Ohio coach, Bob Wren. Amateur coach Ted Mills, on whose semi-pro teams Schmidt participated during his summers home from Athens, credits Wren for possessing the wisdom to advise Schmidt to discontinue switch-hitting. Schmidt had adopted switch-hitting in high school in an effort to hit for a higher average; Wren got Schmidt to abandon it as a sophomore. Schmidt considers it one of the turning points in his career.

"A hitter with the raw power I had can *learn* to hit [for an average]," Schmidt explained. "[But] a hitter who spots the ball cannot *learn* power. Power is God-given. I started switch-hitting in an effort to see fewer curves. Wren said that college pitchers have trouble getting the curve over the plate and that if I laid off them, I would see enough fastballs to become a productive righthanded hitter."

The strides Schmidt accomplished between his freshman and senior years were striking. Frank Morgan, the sports information director at Ohio U., said that he recalls that people started noticing Schmidt as a sophomore. Morgan exchanged his recollections of the "unexplained and explosive power" Schmidt possessed with Ralph Dalton, then the Ohio University groundskeeper. Dalton is 88 now and has a personal letter from Schmidt hanging on his apartment wall.

"He had some pop in his bat," Dalton recalled.

"Wow, did he ever," Morgan said. "That one he hit on top of the Grover Center. That had to be close to a 500-foot job."

"Had to be," Dalton said.

"I hear," Morgan added, "that he hit one to dead center and broke a window in one of the buildings out there."

"Could be," Dalton said. "He hit some towering drives. He hit them so high and far it seemed like they would never come down."

Schmidt himself had come far. He batted .326 in three seasons as a starter at Ohio U. and had 27 home runs, tops on the team. Though the pro scouts who scouted Schmidt still questioned the health of his knees—and expressed that skepticism to their superiors—Phillies scout Tony Lucadello recalls that he noticed Schmidt as a high school sophomore and had been watching him evolve. He remembers seeing both Neff and Schmidt at Fairview and claims that he remembers liking Schmidt.

"The catcher Neff would only get so far," Lucadello says. "Mike seemed to have something."

He searches for the word.

"Class," he decides. "Mike Schmidt had class."

■

Miami of Ohio and Eastern Michigan had a double-header scheduled on this Saturday and Lucadello planned to attend, provided the storms that had threatened Michigan passed to the south. Advised that the weather seemed promising, he drove to Ypsilanti from his Toledo motel and parked his white chevrolet with a view of the field. He still was recovering from the flu and did not want to stand out in the cold.

Lucadello had come to see one of the Miami pitchers, a senior who seemed certain to receive attention in the draft. Lucadello had seen the pitcher earlier in the spring and had not been impressed. Two innings passed and Lucadello remained unimpressed.

"See that?" Lucadello said. "See how he short-arms the ball? He will never pitch in the big leagues. [But] some team will sign him."

Lucadello sighed. "There is not one position player on either team who is a potential big-league player. Not one," Lucadello said. "The talent is diminishing from our sandlots. We have players in the big leagues today who are no better than college players."

Of the 49 players Lucadello has signed who have graduated

to the big leagues—including Fergie Jenkins, Alex Johnson, and pitcher Mike Marshall—none were as intriguing as Schmidt. "He had uncommon power," Lucadello recalls. Though he remembers noting that Schmidt did not appear to have the range to be a big-league shortstop, Lucadello remembers thinking that Schmidt would be a perfect third baseman. Less than three weeks before the 1971 June draft he offered this assessment of Schmidt:

"Looked very good today on defense and at bat . . . showed good hands . . ."

Lucadello recalls that Schmidt "projected" well. "He had that wonderful upper-body strength," Lucadello said. "But I knew we would have to be patient. He would strike out. I knew that. But I also believed he could be a 40-home run man. The essence of scouting is projection. The question I have to answer is this: Will this player one day help us win in the big leagues? I believed [Schmidt] would."

Lucadello placed Schmidt at the top of his draft list and the scout held his breath. The Phillies were only one of the teams that had been high on Schmidt; California had shown some interest but drafted lower. Opting to pursue pitching help, the Phillies drafted sixth and selected Roy Thomas, a California high school pitcher. Thomas is now in the Seattle organization with Triple A Calgary; his career record in the big leagues is 19-11.

The Phillies would have been denied Schmidt were it not for the curious scenario involving the Angels and Frank Tanana, now a pitcher with the Tigers. Tanana had been the top high school pitcher in Michigan in the spring of 1971 and seemed certain to be a high selection. California, drafting 11th, was surprised and delighted that he was still available and selected him, *not knowing* that he had injured his arm some weeks before and would be unable to pitch for more than a year. Had the Angels known that, it is conceivable Schmidt would have been their choice. Scout Carl Ackerman had been enamored of Schmidt and told the *Dayton Journal-Herald* that the Angels were prepared to draft him in the second round.

"I *begged* them to grab Schmidt," Ackerman told the *Herald-Journal*.

The Phillies selected Schmidt with their second-round pick and thus prevented that. Lucadello presented an initial offer of $25,000—one that Jack Schmidt rejected—and then signed Schmidt for $32,500, plus $7,500 in incentive bonuses. Schmidt reported to Reading, hit only .211, but by the next season had been promoted to the big leagues.

Lucadello claims that the career that has followed has been the product of sheer dedication.

"He *knew* what he wanted and he worked at it," Lucadello said. "He practiced. That is the problem today. None of the players today want to *give themselves to the sport* the way he did."

Lucadello turned his head and studied the distance. Eastern Michigan had scored and had runners on second and third base. He continued watching as he started talking.

"Branch Rickey told me something when I was starting out," Lucadello recalled. "We were at a high school diamond one cold spring day and it was the fifth or sixth inning. He asked, 'Are there any players out there that you like?' I told him no. He said, 'Me neither,' and then asked, 'Why are we sitting here in the cold?' "

Lucadello turned his eyes from the field and drove home.

■

School at Northmont High had ended for the day. Dave Palsgrove, still a teacher and a coach, negotiated the crowded halls and unlocked the door to a faculty room. Inside, he placed himself at a table and said: "500 home runs, huh?"

Palsgrove—whom Schmidt regarded as a "second father" —has been at Northmont since Fairview closed seven years ago. Currently the varsity basketball coach, Palsgrove said he started a freshman this season and claims he bears a resemblance to how Palsgrove remembers Schmidt. "You never know [how far he can go]," Palsgrove said, adding that he never would have dreamed that Schmidt would develop into the star that he has become.

"At that point—if I had had to choose between Schmidt and Neff—I would have said Neff [would be a big leaguer]," Palsgrove said. "Shows what I know."

Palsgrove never has been to Cooperstown but he plans to be there on the day Schmidt is inducted into the Hall of

Fame. In a certain way, he is not unlike the other coaches and athletes from that Fairview era in the pride he has for Schmidt. To be able to claim that he contributed to the career of "someone like that" is, for Palsgrove, the high point of his career. Of the hundreds and hundreds of athletes he has coached in 20-odd years—and he has had some excellent ones—none has been as thrilling as Schmidt.

"There is," Palsgrove said, "only *one* Mike Schmidt."

VICTIMS OF THE HOME RUN

BY PAUL DOMOWITCH

It was just one pitch. One pitch out of maybe 40,000 that Ralph Branca threw in the 12 seasons he spent in the big leagues.

But it was the only pitch that mattered. The only pitch of Branca's that history bothered to remember.

It has been almost 36 years since the Giants won the pennant, the Giants won the pennant, the Giants won the pennant. But on a clear day, Branca still can see the ball flying off Bobby Thomson's bat and into the leftfield seats in the Polo Grounds.

"I remember watching it going," Branca said. "I remember standing there on the mound and watching it and hoping like hell it would sink. I was hoping it would hit the wall and not go in [to the stands]. But it did."

There have been other winners and other losers. Other heroes and other goats. But Thomson and Branca are forever linked by the 1951 home run that leaves an indelible impression.

"A guy commits murder and he gets pardoned after 20 years," Branca said. "I didn't get pardoned. I guess this is just something I'm going to have to live with until they put me in the ground.

"After 25 years, I really started to get my fill of it and got hard-nosed about [talking about] it. But then I realized, 'Hey, you're going to live with this until you die. So relax and let it go.'

"I guess the thing that rankles me is that there've been 50 other home runs hit in similar situations and nobody seems to remember them. Nobody talks about Bucky Dent's home run or Jack Clark's or Mazeroski's or Johnny Bench's. Just Thomson's off of me.

"I think Bobby Thomson really came up with it. He said it's because it was New York. Brooklyn and the Giants. Both of us in the media capital of the world and such an intense rivalry for years and years. And, of course, they came from 13 [games] back, too."

Branca had been used mainly as a starter for the Dodgers in 1951. But with two on and one out in the bottom of the ninth and his team clinging to a 4-2 lead, Brooklyn manager Charlie Dressen didn't have any real choice but Branca.

Clem Labin, his best reliever, had pitched nine innings the day before. His other top stopper, Preacher Roe, had a sore arm.

"You know, I loved being a reliever, I truly did," Branca said. "I loved to come in in that situation. It was the best I had felt in six weeks."

His euphoria wouldn't last long. With a 1-2 count on Thomson, Branca threw him a fastball, high and inside. "It was a waste pitch," he said. "I was trying to set him up for the curve. But he kind of guessed me on it."

He guessed and swung and the ball went into the leftfield seats and the Giants won the pennant, the Giants won the pennant, the Giants won the pennant.

Branca never was the same again. He injured his back the next spring, and won just 12 more games over the next three seasons before calling it quits.

"My only regret is that I hurt my back and wasn't able to prove that the homer didn't bother me," Branca said. "I tried too hard to make good after that, and that's how I hurt my back.

"Sports medicine wasn't what it is today where you've got [Dr.] Frank Jobe taking a tendon from Tommy John's wrist and putting it in his elbow. Roger Clemens the same thing. They just weren't sophisticated enough then to help me heal. I wasn't able to throw hard again. I wasn't pitching with a full deck."

■

Like Branca, Ralph Terry also knows what it is like to be

haunted by The Ghost of Home Runs Past. In 1960, the former New York Yankees pitcher gave up probably the second most famous home run of all time. It was the ninth-inning game-winner by the Pirates' Bill Mazeroski in the seventh game of the World Series.

"It's a funny thing, but I'll bet if I live to be 100, somebody will mosey up to me and say, 'What kind of pitch did you throw to Mazeroski?' " said Terry, who now is a golfer on the PGA Senior Tour. "I was hitting balls on the [driving] range this week and Chi Chi Rodriguez saw me. He's a big baseball fan and he hollers over, 'Hey Mazeroski. Hey Maz.'

"Maz's home run was one of those moments that was frozen in time, in history. I've had more people, when they talk about it, tell me exactly what they were doing, where they were at the moment. It's like when [President] Kennedy got shot. Everybody remembers where they were. Same with Maz's homer. It was one of those things that stopped the world for an instant."

Unlike Branca, Terry managed to pick up the pieces and go on. The year after he gave up the Forbes Field home run to Mazeroski, he went 16-3, despite missing six weeks with a sore shoulder. The year after that he won 23 games and pitched the Yanks to a dramatic 1-0 win over the San Francisco Giants in the deciding game of the 1962 World Series.

"Casey Stengel was a big help to me after it happened," Terry said. "We all knew it was going to be his last year [as Yankees manager]. After the game, I said, 'Casey, I'm sorry it had to end this way for you.'

"He said, 'Well, how were you trying to pitch him?' I told him I was trying to throw breaking stuff low and outside and just got one up. He said, 'Well, as long as you pitch, you're not always going to physically be able to get the ball where you want to. But as long as you weren't trying to throw him high fastballs or going against the scouting report, forget it.'

"That meant a lot. To me, Casey was a God in those days. I loved him like a father. I idolized the guy. He was the only guy that could inspire me."

Terry didn't really realize the full effect of Mazeroski's home run on him until after the '62 World Series.

"I went to spring training the year after Mazeroski's homer and everybody was asking me if it was going to bother me," Terry said. "I said, 'Why should it? I'm a young man [he was 24].' It was my first World Series. It was a big thrill for me just being in it. It didn't bother me for a moment. If anything, it might've spurred me on.

"But when I won [the seventh game against the Giants] in '62, I realized it may have bothered me more than I realized. Because I felt a tremendous sense of relief afterward."

■

The most memorable home run Al Downing ever gave up didn't cost his club a pennant or the World Series. It came in April, not October. It came in the fourth game of the season, not the fourth game of the World Series.

It was a home run that wouldn't even have merited a mention on the sports pages were it not for the fact that it was hit by Hank Aaron and was his 715th, which happened to be the one that made him baseball's all-time leading home run hitter.

Downing pitched 17 years in the major leagues. He won 123 games, including 20 in 1971 with the Dodgers. He appeared in three World Series and four All-Star games. Yet, nine out of 10 people remember Downing best for the home run he gave up to Aaron.

"It depends on what part of the country you're from," said Downing, who now works in the Dodgers' community relations department. "The people of New York [he spent nine years with the Yankees] don't relate to that as much. I don't know why. I was in New York last summer and the only thing the people wanted to talk about were the '60s.

"Yet, on the West Coast, the only thing people remember are my years with the Dodgers and the home run.

"Granted, it was a historic moment in baseball and I'm not trying to belittle it. But it's not the kind of thing you go around every day thinking about. There are World Series games that had far more effect on me than that game. Anybody could've been on the mound that night."

■

Anybody could have been on the mound in Yankee Stadium on Sept. 30, 1961, the day Roger Maris hit his 61st home run of the season to break Babe Ruth's mark. Anybody. But the pitcher was Tracy Stallard.

"I've met a million people who said they were there that day and I think they only had 23,000 for that game," said Stallard, a 6-5, 204-pound righthander from the Blue Ridge Mountains who spent six fairly nondescript years in the majors pitching for Boston, St. Louis, and the Mets. "If I hadn't have done that [given up the homer to Maris], nobody'd probably remember my name right now. So I guess it's better than nothing.

"I tried my best to get him out. But I could've struck him out four times that day and that wouldn't have meant anything. I'm glad he did it. He deserved it. I think it'll be a record that'll stand for a long, long time. At least as long as I'm alive."

Aaron hit his milestone home run the second time up against Downing that night. The first time up, much to the displeasure of the Atlanta crowd, Downing walked him. Then, in the fourth inning, he tried to come in with a knee-high fastball, but got it up.

"It's funny," Downing said. "Three years ago, on the 10th anniversary of Hank's homer, we re-enacted it in Atlanta. They had me pitch to him until he hit one out. It took 18 pitches. That's why I laugh when people say, 'Gee, you must have grooved that pitch to him [in 1974].'

"I said, 'Groove it? Three years ago, I went out there trying to let him hit it out and it took 18 pitches.' That's just baseball."

HOME RUN HEYDAY

BY BERNARD FERNANDEZ

The comparison of baseball statistics is among the most subjective of topics, although certain career numbers always have been above debate. Attain one of those magic figures and a player should expect enshrinement in the Hall of Fame.

"There are no specific guidelines, but if somebody gets 3,000 hits or 500 home runs or 300 wins, he ought to be in there," Phillies broadcaster Rich Ashburn, a standout centerfielder on the 1950 Whiz Kids, said in outlining the more widely accepted criteria for admission to Cooperstown. "It ought to be automatic."

Phillies superstar Mike Schmidt entered his 15th full major league season with 495 career homers. And now he has crossed the threshold of 500 home runs, a barrier that presumably assures baseball immortality. Now 37 and coming off his third MVP season, Schmidt ranks ninth on the all-time home run list. Conceivably, he could surpass 600 career homers if he plays for another three seasons at his current level of productivity. Only three players—legendary Hall of Famers Henry Aaron (755), Babe Ruth (714), and Willie Mays (660)—can claim that distinction.

"I would think Mike is an automatic pick [for the Hall of Fame]," Rocky Colavito, a noted slugger of the 1950s and '60s, said of Schmidt. "Five-hundred home runs is a lot of home runs. If you don't think so, just check and see how exclusive a club that is. You're talking about a great, great feat."

Great feat, no doubt. But Schmidt's power totals would be even more impressive if he had played his entire career in, say, Wrigley Field, a long-ball hitter's haven. Schmidt has swatted 47 home runs as a visiting player at Wrigley.

"If Mike had played half his games in Wrigley Field all this time," Ashburn said, "he wouldn't be just past breaking 500. He would be on the verge of breaking Aaron's record."

The might-have-beens always have sparked discussions among fans who like to project what a certain player would have accomplished under different circumstances. What kind of numbers might Mickey Mantle have posted if he had had two good knees? Or if Ted Williams had not lost nearly five of his prime years to military service? Would Ruth have been as dominant in a later era, after the introduction of night games, overpowering relief specialists, and the split-fingered fastball?

Two power hitters of another generation—Colavito and Orlando Cepeda—say Schmidt would have produced high home run totals at any point in baseball history.

"Mike Schmidt is one hell of a home run hitter," said Colavito, 53, who ended his career with 374 home runs, including seven seasons of 30 or more. "He's put up consistently good numbers over a period of time. That's the real test. Some guys do it for a couple of years, but they don't hold up over the long haul."

"Schmidt, [Don] Mattingly, [Jim] Rice . . . guys like that would be outstanding hitters in any era," said Cepeda, 49, who had five seasons of 30-plus homers in a 17-year career that ended in 1974. "Mike is a true home-run hitter—one of the best ever."

Colavito and Cepeda can't help but wonder what Schmidt might have achieved had he played during their careers in the '50s and '60s, an era that spawned an inordinately large number of long-ball threats.

The late 1950s and early 1960s. It was a time of small ballparks, short fences and big boppers who struck fear into the heart of opposing pitchers. Never was the home run more commonplace than in 1961, a season in which eight players pounded 40 or more balls into the stands.

Roger Maris, of course, led the long-ball brigade with his

record 61 homers. Joining him as American League members of the 40-plus club were Mantle, his New York Yankees teammate, with 54; Harmon Killebrew, of the Minnesota Twins (46); Jim Gentile, of the Baltimore Orioles (46); Colavito, of the Detroit Tigers (45); and Norm Cash, of the Tigers (41).

Cepeda, of the San Francisco Giants, led the National League that season with 46 homers. Willie Mays, his teammate, had 40.

Among the vaunted sluggers who did not make it to 40 in '61 were Aaron (34), Frank Robinson (37) and Ernie Banks (29).

Led by the Milwaukee Braves with 188, the eight NL teams walloped 1,196 homers in 1961, an average of 149.5 per team. The 10 AL teams exceeded that total with 1,534 homers. With the Yankees racking up a record 240, the AL average was 153.4 per team.

"I think maybe you had more prolific home run hitters playing then than at any time in the game's history," Colavito said. "A lot of home runs were being hit, and the guys who hit them were no fly-by-nighters. They were players who hit a lot of home runs over the course of their careers.

"Oh, every now and then somebody comes along who has a freaky kind of season. I remember Davey Johnson hitting over 40 home runs one season for the Atlanta Braves. There's a guy who never hit 40 home runs in his life—not before, not after. But the people who hit a lot of home runs in 1961, for the most part, were the real thing."

Cepeda said there was such an abundance of home run hitters in the late '50s and early '60s that a number of good hitters with pop in their bats were widely overlooked.

"If somebody hit 27 or 28 homers, nobody said much about it because it wasn't that unusual," Cepeda said. "I remember Johnny Callison [a former Phillie] and George Altman [of the Chicago Cubs]. They'd always be in the high 20s [in home runs], but you never heard anyone talk about them as being home-run hitters.

"In those days, big home-run hitters were the big stars. If you didn't hit home runs, [management] didn't think you were anything. I remember a guy from the Dominican Republic named Manny Jimenez, who was one of the best hitters I ever saw. One year he was hitting something like .352 at the All-Star break [for Kansas City] and Hank Bauer, his manager, always was criticizing him in the papers because he didn't hit the long ball. But he hit 11 or 12 homers that year. Today, that would be considered pretty good."

Cepeda said the older, smaller ballparks that most teams called home in the early 1960s helped inflate home-run totals.

"Philadelphia [Veterans Stadium] is a good park for a hitter, but Connie Mack Stadium was better," Cepeda said. "The parks they have now in Cincinnati, Pittsburgh, and St. Louis aren't as good for the hitter as the old ones were. All the new parks help the pitcher."

Ashburn, a line-drive hitter who had 29 career homers in 15 seasons, agreed with Cepeda.

"Forget about Wrigley Field," Ashburn said. "If Schmidt had played his entire career in our old ballpark [Connie Mack], where the ball carried well and the fences were short in left and left-center, he'd have a lot more homers than he has now. And that's not even taking into consideration good home run parks that aren't there any longer, like Crosley Field in Cincinnati.

"I think the emphasis is still very much on power, but not to the extent it was in the '50s and '60s. Back then, power was important almost to a fault. It took a pretty good whack to knock it out of Sportsman's Park in St. Louis, but at least it was easier than the place they play in now [Busch Memorial Stadium].

"But I don't want to make it sound like the ballparks were the only reason so many home runs were hit back then. I don't think there's ever been an era that produced so many consistently good power hitters. You might say it was a gathering of eagles."

In 1961, Schmidt was an 11-year-old growing up in Dayton, Ohio. He was a fan of the Cincinnati Reds, whose power-laden lineup included Robinson, Vada Pinson, Gordy Coleman, Gene Freese, and Wally Post. Even then, might Little Leaguer Schmidt have been influenced to swing for the fences?

"I don't think what you see when you're growing up has

any bearing on what you become," Schmidt said. "It has more to do with other things—your body build, for example. If you're tall and lefthanded, you're probably going to become a pitcher, not a third baseman."

Fair enough. But has Schmidt ever wondered about what it might be like to play an entire career in Wrigley Field, or to have come along in an era when power was a player's primary asset and small parks were the rule rather than the exception?

"I always have a problem with that question," Schmidt said. "How many home runs would I have hit if I had played in the Astrodome? There's no sense in conjecture. The good Lord put me in this role on this team at this time. It's up to me to use that platform to make my mark."

Schmidt has used that platform very well. Five-hundred home runs is an achievement of such stature that each of the 14 players in the 500-homer club—with the exception of Reggie Jackson, who is still active—has been voted into the Hall of Fame.

While endorsing Schmidt as Hall of Fame material, Cepeda said it is Ashburn who might be the Phillie most adversely affected by the era in which he played.

"Richie was a great player," Cepeda said. "He'd hit .330, .335 every year and nobody mentioned him as a superstar because he didn't hit home runs. But he was a superstar. He could run, he could field, he could hit.

"If Richie played today, with all these big ballparks and artificial turf, he'd hit .350 every year and make a million dollars."

Ashburn appreciates the kind words, but he remembers something former Pittsburgh Pirates slugger Ralph Kiner once said: Singles-hitters drive Fords, home-run hitters drive Cadillacs.

"The guy sitting in the stands is in awe of the guy on the field who can hit the long ball," Ashburn said. "That's the way it was, the way it is, and the way it'll probably always be."

Rave Reviews: We read them all and review the best.

Subscribe to the exciting magazine of popular fiction. Each information packed issue includes over 100 reviews and news of:

- Contemporary
- Thriller
- Historical
- Mystery
- Romance
- Horror
- S F /Fantasy
- NonFiction

☐ Enclosed is a check or money order for 10.95 for 1 year (6 issues) of Rave Reviews.

FREE BOOK OFFER FOR NEW SUBSCRIBERS
Circle one of the above categories and we will send you a FREE book.

Name_____
Addres_____
City_____ State_____ Zip_____
Rave Reviews, 163 Joralemon St., Brooklyn Hgts., NY 11201